COPYRIGHT INFORMATION

This is a book of fiction, set during 1765 in historic Williamsburg, Virginia. Most of the major characters in the book are factual and while the author has attempted to make the dialogue match what we know about the characters' history, all dialogue is fictional and the specific murder described is also fictional. Several characters in the book are not real or are placed in different positions than actual and are used to further the story. Most of the specific events in the book did not occur. The general historical information is correct although the author has taken liberty with some of the details, including specific dates and times of the action. All the conclusions and political thinking of the characters are invented by the author and not historical fact.

DEDICATION

This book is dedicated to my soulmate and spouse Suzanne Erlon Kee and to the staff and interpreters of The Colonial Williamsburg Foundation, who make history come alive.

TABLE OF CONTENTS

CAST OF MAIN CHARACTERS

William Norvell, Sheriff of Williamsburg and James City County

George Wythe, lawyer and Member of the House of Burgesses
    Elizabeth, his wife
    Thomas Jefferson, his law clerk and a plantation owner
    Luck Key, his junior clerk
    Lydia (Liddy) Broadnax, housekeeper and cook

James Johnson, Member of the House of Burgesses from King William County, plantation owner
    Sarah, his wife
    Bethany, his daughter
    John Mechem, plantation overseer

John Minson Galt, Doctor and Apothecary owner; and City and County Coroner

Lt. Governor Francis Fauquier

John Robinson, Speaker of the House of Burgesses
    Susanna Chiswell, his wife
    Edmund Chiswell, his brother-in-law, a Burgesses from Middlesex County

Other Members of the House of Burgesses in 1765:
    Carter Braxton, from King William County
    Patrick Henry, from Louisa County
    Richard Henry Lee, from Prince William County
    John Page, from Gloucester County
    Peyton Randolph, Attorney General or Kings Attorney, from Williamsburg
    Robert Carter III, plantation owner, lawyer and member of the

Governor's Council.

Williamsburg Merchants:
  James Anderson, Blacksmith
  Josiah Chowning, owner, Chowning's Tavern
  James Craig, Silversmith
  James Geddy, Silversmith
  Anthony Hay, owner, Raleigh Tavern
  George Wilson, Shoemaker

Others:

Jacob, slave previously owned by Mr. Johnson and now by the blacksmith James Anderson. Jacob's wife Sally.

Mrs. Julia George, owner of a guest house in Williamsburg
Mrs. Lucy McIntyre, owner of a guest house in Williamsburg

CHAPTER 1

Sunday May 19

The spring night was warmer than usual, but without the high humidity common in the south. After a fortnight of rain, it was a pleasure to see just a few clouds in the clearing skies; night hawks filled the night air as they swooped in on their winged prey. James Johnson walked up Nassau Street in Williamsburg and by Burton Parish Church on the Duke of Gloucester Street, passing several closed shops including the shoemaker's house. He walked onto the square housing the Powder Magazine, which contained the armaments and powder of the Virginia militia.

It was Sunday and he had expected to see no one out at this time of night. Chowning's Tavern, across the street, was quiet and he was a fair distance from the more rowdy taverns further down the street. He could still hear some sounds emanating from that direction, but no one was out on the street and so as expected he was alone.

Johnson was a careful man. He was a farmer and descendant from an early founder of Virginia, a so-called "ancient planter," someone who survived the Indian Massacre in 1622 and continued to maintain a home in Virginia. His friends had a good opinion of him and he was thought of as one of his county's community leaders. He had a wife whom he loved and a daughter that was loved by both of them. Why then did he find himself walking to the Williamsburg Powder Magazine at near midnight on this May 19 night?

Johnson supposed the facts were simple. He was in town for the 1765 sessions of the Virginia House of Burgesses, a representative from King William County, and he was in financial difficulty, as were many of his fellow plantation owners. But he had learned a secret, which might give him an advantage in his business affairs, if he played his cards right. He was not sure about the possible risk but judged it manageable.

As he entered the enclosed walls, he saw the octagonal brick Magazine in the dim star-light—the new moon providing little additional light. An owl screeched as it attacked its prey; otherwise all was quiet. No one seemed to be present, but there was a faint glow of a lantern streaming from the partially opened door of the Magazine. He called out, but received no response. He was not overly concerned as he expected to find the door open, but he took out his small pistol, just in case he needed it.

He opened the door further, hearing the faint squeak of its hinges, and stepped into the large open area of the Magazine. As he walked in, he felt someone at his back and started to turn around. He suddenly felt a sharp, stabbing pain in his shoulder and back. He lost his balance and fell to the dirt floor. His last thoughts were of his wife and daughter as he lost consciousness.

CHAPTER 2

Monday May 20

Luck Key was feeling fortunate this fine spring morning in 1765. The sun had just risen and it looked like it was going to be a beautiful day. He was eighteen and last month was released as an apprentice to William Byers of Augusta County Virginia. The Luisa County Court had placed Luck and his brothers in apprentice positons at the request of his mother Elizabeth, after their father had died. As an apprentice he worked alongside both free men and slaves who worked on the Byers planation. In return, Byers provided a shared room and food. Byers was supposed to provide overall guidance to Luck, though without the emotional attachment of a father.

He liked Byers and learned a great deal about farming from him. Luck's father Martin Key was a farmer before his death, but his farm was quite small compared to Byers' farm and the Key family had done most of the work. Luck thought the experience of working for Byers would benefit him if he also became a farmer. It was not a life he particularly wanted to live and he was here in Williamsburg looking for other options.

The estate of his father had recently been settled following the death of his mother Elizabeth and he was the beneficiary of a small inheritance. Most importantly, he had just been given the opportunity to work with one of Williamsburg's most prominent citizens and a member of the House of

Burgesses, George Wythe, as his junior clerk. He had met Mr. Wythe during the estate settlement and had brashly asked him whether a position of clerk was available in his law offices. Luck had little formal education, but he was thankful that both his father and mother insisted that he learn Latin and English grammar and rhetoric, along with history and math. He had told Mr. Wythe that he was a quick learner, had excellent handwriting and provided the references of William Byers and his uncle Peter Burford.

George Wythe told Luck that he had many previous dealings with his uncle Peter Burford and, after a consultation with him, Wythe had made an offer to Luck of a position as a junior clerk—on a trial basis. Wythe's senior law clerk was Thomas Jefferson who was nearly finished with his law studies; Wythe knew he would need someone new to assist him. Luck thought that George Wythe seemed to like him and so was willing to give Luck a chance. Luck was astonished and excited about the prospect.

Because the House of Burgesses was in session in Williamsburg, the city bulged from its normal sleepy population of a little over 1,000 to twice that number. Luck was fortunate to have found a place to sleep the previous night just outside of the town center and was still in need of finding more permanent lodgings. He had dressed up for his first day of work in clean tan breaches, a white shirt, white wool stockings, and his only good pair of shoes, hoping to present a suitable impression.

He intended to be at Wythe's house at seven o'clock. Luck walked with a slight limp as he was born with a club foot. However, exercises when he was young alleviated some of the distortion and he had learned to adjust his shoes to strengthen the weakness so, though he could not run, he could still walk fairly quickly. But since he had time he strolled by the stately Capitol Building and down the Duke of Gloucester Street, a wide east-west expanse nearly one hundred feet across with the Capitol Building at one end and the College of William and Mary about a mile at the other end of the street.

He had never been to a town the size and importance of
Williamsburg. He had made one trip when he was a boy
with his father to Norfolk, which was becoming one of the
most prosperous cities in Virginia. Norfolk was Virginia's
shipbuilding center and a port city that exported goods
like tobacco, corn, cotton, and timber from Virginia and
other southern colonies and imported manufactured goods
from Britain and other European countries. But Norfolk
was dirty and undeveloped compared to Williamsburg
and Luck was in awe of his new surroundings.

He marveled at the shops and taverns along the way
wondering what famous people were staying here because of
the legislative season. He expected Thomas Jefferson might
be in Williamsburg. Though he was not a member of the
House of Burgesses, he was studying law with Mr. Wythe. Luck
was from Louisa County and some of his family had business
with the Jeffersons from the adjacent Albermarle County and
they had spoken highly about the young Tom Jefferson.

Since he was from Louisa County, there also was a lot of buzz
about Patrick Henry, the county's new member of the House,
a lawyer and firebrand who had been inflaming the public
about the injustices of the proposed Stamp Act of Parliament.

Undoubtedly many members of the House of Burgesses
were just arising for the day, perhaps ready to have breakfast
at one of the many taverns along the main and side streets
including the Raleigh Tavern, the Kings Arms Tavern,
Shield's Tavern, Chowning's Tavern and others that he
noted along this walk. He wondered whether he would
have the money someday to be able to afford to dine in one
of the better places. His landlady had provided him in the
morning with a simple breakfast of sliced meat and corn
bread—more than enough for Luck's tastes and needs.

Mr. Wythe had told Luck that his house was on the west
side of the Palace Green, just north of the Duke of Gloucester
Street, a short walk from the Governor's Palace, and about
half way between the Capitol Building and the College of

William and Mary. Luck walked by many lovely homes and could see the well-kept gardens that graced the rear of the houses. The scent of the flowers made for a pleasant walk. However, it made him miss his mother Elizabeth who so loved the flowers she planted by their home. Most of the houses were two story brick or wood structures and all seemed to be well cared for. Did owners especially paint and fix things up when the House of Burgesses was in session? Luck thought probably not; he expected their owners kept up the property regardless of whether the Burgesses were in session.

As he passed the village square, he saw the Powder Magazine on his left. It was an unusual two story octagonal structure surrounded by a five-foot high brick wall, with one entry point. His father had been in Williamsburg during the French and Indian Wars and had seen the Magazine, describing it to Luck and explaining its role for the Virginia Militia. Since Luck had a little time before he was due at Mr. Wythe's house, he thought he would take a quick look at the structure and walked through the opening in the wall.

Luck noticed that the door to the Powder Magazine itself was ajar. This puzzled Luck, as the Magazine contained the armaments and powder for the Virginia Militia, and obviously the door should not have been open inviting theft or mischief. What should he do? He was naturally inquisitive and had a strong sense of responsibility instilled by his parents. He felt he had time and a duty to inspect the Magazine and see if anything was amiss.

He entered the Magazine and was immediately struck by a powerful smell—a pungent odor that seemed strangely metallic and at the same time sickly unpleasant—perhaps like rotting fruit. As light filtered through the door and window slots, Luck saw a man on the floor; blood had poured out of a wound to his shoulder and back. Quickly Luck knelt down and felt for a pulse in the poor man's neck and found none; the man's limbs were already starting to stiffen. He was uncertain what to do or whom to call and thought that his only possible action was to report this to George Wythe immediately. This was clearly not an accident.

He stumbled out of the door of the Magazine, feeling nauseous and light headed. Getting his bearings he hurried as fast as he could the two blocks to the Wythe home and went to the back door of the main house, assuming someone would be awake and preparing the table for breakfast. He knocked on the door and waited for a response. Only then did he realize that he was sweating profusely, his hair was out of place and his newly pressed white shirt had blood on the sleeves.

CHAPTER 3

ythe's Negro housekeeper Lydia (Liddy) Broadnax opened the door and stared at the young man who now looked quite unkempt and had blood on his shirt. "Good gracious young man, who are you and what have you done?" she screamed.

"I am Luck Key, the new junior clerk of Mr. Wythe," said Luck, trying to compose himself as best he could. "Please tell him I am here and have some awful news, there has been a murder."

Lydia left Luck at the back porch and hurried upstairs to find Mr. Wythe, who was just finishing his dressing. "Master, please come immediately! There is a young man at the back door who claims he is your new junior clerk and I think he has murdered someone! There is blood on his shirt."

Wythe calmed Liddy down, took leave of his wife Elizabeth, and went downstairs to the back door, opening it for Luck. He invited Luck into the foyer, asking him, "What have you to say for yourself young man?"

Luck hurriedly related his grisly find in the Powder Magazine and bade Wythe to come with him to see for himself. Wythe told Liddy to go find Doctor John Galt, who also was the city and county coroner, either at his home or the Apothecary and ask him to meet Wythe at the Magazine.

They all left and a short time later Wythe and Luck reached the Magazine. They went inside and Wythe asked Luck if the body and Magazine were exactly as he had originally discovered it. Luck said yes, nothing had changed. A short time later the doctor joined them and viewed the carnage. Wythe asked Luck to stand outside the door to make sure no one interrupted them.

"As you can see, *rigor mortis* has already set in," the doctor said. "This means he was likely killed sometime last night, at least several hours ago." Galt was trained at the Saint Thomas Hospital in London, and while he was in charge of the local Apothecary, he handled many medical issues for the residents and visitors of Williamsburg. "Who is he?"

Wythe and Galt carefully lifted the dead man, who though not tall was stout, and turned him over on his back. "My heavens," Wythe exclaimed, "this is James Johnson from King William County, a representative in the House of Burgesses. I just saw him this past week. Who could have done this to him?"

Wythe immediately told Galt that he felt that they could rule out Luck as a suspect. "My new junior clerk was on the way to my home this morning and saw the Magazine door open and went to investigate. Johnson had obviously been dead for hours when he found him and it seems unlikely that Luck even knew who Johnson was, as he has come from Louisa County and has never been in Williamsburg before today."

"It also looks like someone has gone through the dead man's pockets," said Wythe. "I wonder what they were searching for. Perhaps something that would link Mr. Johnson to the murderer. We need to contact the Sheriff. Do you have any idea where he is now?" Wythe asked the doctor. "I have not seen him in town for the session."

"I think he may be in Jamestown," replied Doctor Galt. "You may know the county sheriffs have been asked by Governor Fauquier to determine the likely compliance by Virginia's counties with the Stamp Tax, now under consideration by Parliament. I think Sheriff Norvell was checking with the political leadership in Jamestown. I know he has been talking about this issue to people in Williamsburg."

They went outside of the Magazine and Wythe said to Mr. Key, "Luck, if I provide you a horse, can you quickly ride to Jamestown and find Sheriff Norvell."

"Yes sir, I am a good rider and I know that if I follow the southern path out of town it will take me to Jamestown, where I can inquire about the Sheriff."

"Come back to my house," said Wythe, "and clean up. I will write a note to the Sheriff, explaining the circumstances and asking that he return with you to Williamsburg as soon as possible."

Doctor Galt said that as coroner he had seen everything that he needed to see and suggested that they should move the body to a shed behind his Apothecary, which he used as a temporary morgue. "I don't think we should leave the body here. It is warm and it is already creating a strong smell." Wythe agreed. "Doctor please take care of the body as you suggested and also have someone cordon off and guard this area so that it is not disturbed before the Sheriff has a chance to see for himself the murder scene." The doctor immediately took charge of the scene of the crime while Key and Wythe returned to Wythe's home.

A change of shirt later, borrowed from Wythe, Luck took the letter that Wythe had prepared for the Sheriff, mounted the horse provided for him, and left. He had not been on a horse of this quality very often and was glad to have a chance for a fast ride to Jamestown even if burdened with the horrific news.

CHAPTER 4

Sheriff William Norvell was eating a late breakfast at Jamestown Tavern and enjoying a bit of a break from his business responsibilities. He was 40 years of age and had been Sheriff of Williamsburg and James City County since 1757. He was widely respected and not much escaped his attention. Norvell was a widower, his wife Rebecca having died in child-birth along with their second child; their first child, a daughter Johanna, was in England at school. Thus he felt little reason to stay at his small plantation on the James River except on week-ends or holidays. He enjoyed being in town during the week, chatting with the merchants and testing the temperature of the people.

While modest in demeanor, Norvell knew that there were few people in the county who had the degree of executive and administrative powers as he had as Sheriff. In theory, sheriffs served both the county and the English crown and he was appointed by the King's Representative—the Governor. In practice, he served at the recommendations of the elite of the county, the planters and other business interests. Not that he was unwilling to challenge them at times, but his continued appointment as Sheriff depended upon their good will and recommendations to the Governor.

He had extensive legal and financial responsibilities. As the chief peace officer he had the full rights of *posse comitatus*, the right to deputize civilians in the pursuit of a criminal, and he was responsible for arrests and forwarding his recommendations to the county courts. He also was in charge of the operations and maintenance of the Goal or jail, where miscreants were kept for trial or for their eventual punishment. The Sheriff was the collector of taxes for the colony, county and parish. He was also the master of elections, charged with ensuring that they were conducted fairly. Given all of his duties, he had the ability to reward his friends with patronage; thus he was well regarded and influential in the community.

Norvell felt that there was increasing tension and concern from many people about the Stamp Act and other actions of Parliament. Tempers were rising, but many residents supported the King and the ability of Parliament to pass laws affecting the colonies. Everyone including Norvell hoped that cool heads would prevail and that there could be some mutual accommodation. Most people liked the current representative of the Crown, Lieutenant Governor Francis Fauquier, who was generally supportive of the positions of the House of Burgesses.

However, the proposed Stamp Act was not popular as it would place a small charge on every legal paper in the colonies. So instead of levying a tax on trade, which was widely accepted as within Parliament's authority, this would be a direct tax on products used by the people living in Virginia and the other colonies. The threat was that no paper would be legal without the official stamp. Like many he talked to, he was not happy about the proposed tax and glad that he would not be the one required to collect it, as that would fall to a special representative appointed by the Crown.

He was just finishing his breakfast of chicken, hot corn bread, and marmalade. He liked to drink his coffee with a bit of rum in the mornings, preferring that to ale that others often drank with their breakfast. Into the tavern burst an agitated young man that Norvell did not know asking for the Sheriff. Norvell motioned the young man over to his table. "Come here young man, this instant, what is all the anxiety about?"

"Good day sir," said Luck, "are you the Sheriff?" Norvell

nodded that he was. "I have been asked by my master George Wythe to give you this message." Key handed over the note written by Wythe. Norvell read the message, which briefly explained the events in Williamsburg and asked Norvell to return with Mr. Key as soon as possible to take charge of the investigation.

"Well, I guess we had better be off then," the Sheriff said as he stood up from the table. Key noticed that Sheriff Norvell was a tall man, over six feet tall and well built, with penetrating blue-grey eyes and a commanding presence. "My horse is tied up outside and we can leave immediately. Have you had anything to eat?" Hearing Key indicate that he had not, Sheriff Norvell asked the tavern owner to make a meal for Mr. Key for the road and settled his bill.

Luck was surprised and grateful to the Sheriff for thinking about his needs despite the situation.

CHAPTER 5

The eight mile trip back to Williamsburg took a bit longer than one and a half hours by horse and the road wound itself through some of the most beautiful forest land in Virginia. During the ride, the Sheriff questioned Mr. Key on what he knew about the situation. Luck explained his new position as junior clerk with Mr. Wythe. His father had once described the Powder Magazine to him and, since it was on his way to the Wythe house, he had time to take a quick look at it. When he saw the door to the Powder Magazine ajar he decided to see why it was open.

"Why didn't you go directly to Wythe's house? What made you go into the Magazine?" asked the Sheriff.
"I was just curious," said Key. "I suppose I might have let it go, but it just did not seem right that the door was left open. Something was wrong. I had a few minutes before my reporting to Mr. Wythe so I thought I would try to discover if anything was amiss. Perhaps that was not the best judgment, but that is what I decided to do."

"Tell me everything you noticed in the Magazine," said Norvell.

"Well I did see if the man was still alive—he was not of course," said Key, "and unfortunately I got some of the dead man's blood on my shirt. It was fairly dark in the Magazine. I did notice the wound, because the man was lying on his front and the wound was on his shoulder and back. It seemed to be a slash, which might have been caused by a halberd or ax, rather than a stab, as if he had been killed by a knife or sword. That was about all I noticed, as I then went to see Mr. Wythe and returned with him. The doctor arrived shortly thereafter and Mr. Wythe asked me to go outside to prevent anyone from coming into the Magazine while they did a preliminary investigation."

Sheriff Norvell and Key arrived in Williamsburg at midday. Luck went to the Wythe house and the Sheriff headed to the Magazine. Luck knocked on Wythe's back door and reported to him that he had come back to Williamsburg with the Sheriff, who was at the Magazine. Wythe told one of his servants to take charge of the horse and they went out of the house and walked over to the Magazine. A crowd had gathered. Doctor Galt had removed the body from the Magazine to a makeshift morgue behind the Apothecary.

The Magazine was guarded by one of the doctor's assistants, who had not gone inside the Magazine. Norvell nodded to the man, who recognized the Sheriff, and told Norvell that he had kept everyone out on the doctor's instructions. He stepped aside to let the Sheriff go inside. Shortly thereafter, Wythe and Key arrived, and when Norvell heard them speaking to the doctor's assistant, he asked for them to come inside and again requested a brief description of what each person had done and seen.

Luck repeated what he had told the Sheriff on the journey and could think of no further details. Wythe explained that after Mr. Key had told him his story he had sent for the doctor and they had viewed the body. Since *rigor mortis* was already advancing, with the limbs stiffening, the doctor had concluded that the death had occurred sometime late on Sunday night or early Monday morning.

He asked them to help him search for a possible murder weapon, noting that Mr. Key had suggested that an ax or halberd, with its hatchet-like blade, might be the weapon. Carefully the men searched the Magazine, both the ground floor and the upper floor where powder was stored. The Magazine contained a variety of weapons: sabers, pikes, halberds, and muskets, as well as powder.

Luck called out, "I think there is something here." Pointing behind a barrel of powder they saw a bloodied halberd of the type once used a great deal in battles by common soldiers, but now not as much, as men relied more on their muskets and swords. The halberd was a tall weapon with a sharpened point at the end, like a pike. But halberds also had a hatchet-like blade at the end of the weapon before the point. Thus the weapon could be used both to stab and to slash at the enemy. The blood on the sharp hatchet-like blade suggested to the three men that this likely was the weapon used to kill James Johnson.

Norvell also looked around on the dirt floor to see if there were any other signs of the person or persons involved or any other evidence. "Look here," pointed out Norvell, "there appears to be boot prints behind the door. It is hard to see the prints as the floor is quite firm, but it is definitely a boot and probably a man's boot. There also appears to be some tobacco stains by the door. Perhaps also used by the assailant," said the Sheriff.

Wythe and Key examined the two items and agreed on the boots probably being a man's, but there was not enough of a print to try to determine a size. The tobacco stain did not seem fresh and perhaps was made by someone other than the assailant.

In a far corner Wythe noticed a small pistol—obviously not the murder weapon. "I wonder if the pistol was James Johnson's?" asked Wythe. "If so, it suggests that Johnson was at least somewhat concerned for his safety."

Thanking Wythe and Key, Sheriff Norvell took what evidence they had and walked over to the Apothecary to speak to Dr. Galt, the city and county coroner. "Let's look at the body," said Norvell, "and tell me what you think." Galt took Norvell in back to look at the body. He had met James Johnson and surely this was the man, although now bloated and beginning to blacken. Galt pointed out the slashing wound on the upper right shoulder and

running down the back, which was sufficient to pierce
the lungs and heart, breaking thought the rib cage.

"This obviously took considerable force to make
this wound," said the Sheriff. "A man?"
"In all probability," said the doctor. "I don't see how a
women could exert this type of force. And it looks like the
blow was at a downward angle. Johnson though stout was
not a tall man, but I expect our murderer was quite tall,
given the nature of the downward arc of the wound."

"Yes, I think the evidence and the likely murder
weapon point to a man," said Norvell.
Dr. Galt was a physician and as the city and county
coroner it was his responsibility to hold the inquest and
determine the nature of the death. In this case the cause
was clear, though the perpetrator was unknown.

"I would suggest a five man panel for the inquest," said Dr.
Galt, "Would you ask George Wythe and have him enlist
four others for the task. It seems to me that we could hold
the inquest quite soon, perhaps Thursday afternoon. We
obviously need to inform the family first and allow them
the opportunity to provide any information on why Mr.
Johnson was at the Magazine in the middle of the night."

Norvell nodded his agreement and suggested Thursday
at 4 pm for the inquest. "I will talk to Mr. Wythe now
and ask him to select the inquest jury and then I will
ride to King William County to see Mr. Johnson's family
and give them the unfortunate news." said Norvell.
"Would you please take charge of the evidence for
the Johnson Inquest?" Dr. Galt agreed to do so.

Norvell walked to the Wythe house thinking about the
situation. James Johnson's murder appeared unusual and
potentially explosive as he was a member of the House of
Burgesses. Why was he there? Was he investigating the open
door as Mr. Key did this morning or, more likely, was he
meeting someone there? What enemies had he made, either in
business, his personal life or politics? Whose pistol did they

find? If Johnson's, had he feared for his life, or did he take it merely as a precaution. It looked like Johnson was surprised as he entered the Magazine and struck from behind. There was no evidence of a fight. The use of a halberd as a murder weapon also was somewhat surprising. It was a weapon used by unskilled rank and file soldiers but now largely unused as more people had access to muskets. Was it used because the murderer was unskilled in other weapons? Or had the person used the weapon to confuse potential investigators and put suspicions on others? "Too many questions!" thought Norvell.

Sheriff Norvell considered George Wythe, who he knew, but not well. He was regarded as one of the finest attorneys in Virginia and a man of unimpeachable integrity. He and his wife Elizabeth were fixtures in the social scene at Governor's Balls and other events. Norvell would describe Wythe as about medium height, wiry and trim. He had a high forehead, well-arched eyebrows and a "Roman" nose that complemented a somewhat enlarged head—all needed to contain his vast sources of knowledge—or so it was said. He also had penetrating blue eyes that reflected both his well-regarded intelligence and his kindness and benevolence when dealing both with his clients and people in general. In addition, unlike most Virginians, who seldom bathed, Wythe showered outside daily with cold water and maintained a daily physical exercise regime. The overall effect was a healthy, vibrant manner that he carried off with little fuss or regard for how others might see him.

When Norvell arrived he explained to Mr. Wythe that Dr. Galt asked if he would find four others to serve with him on the inquest jury. "I would suggest Tom Jefferson," said Wythe. "He is studying law in my offices and is a fellow plantation owner. I don't believe he has any connections to Mr. Johnson and thus would be an impartial member. I will also ask two fellow members of the House of Burgesses and perhaps one of the town merchants."

"That certainly is acceptable to me," said Norvell. "Please

ask them and arrange the details with Dr. Galt. I also have
a favor to ask of you," continued the Sheriff to Wythe.
"My under-sheriff is away on an extended trip to England
because of a death in the family and some estate issues.
So I find myself rather shorthanded for this investigation.
Would you allow me to borrow Mr. Key, your junior clerk?
He seems quite observant and sharp. I could use someone to
help me take notes of my interviews and perhaps provide a
different perspective. Would that be acceptable to you?"

Wythe thought about it for a moment and then agreed.
"Of course you have the right to deputize anyone for this
investigation, pursuant to law. However, I am glad that you
asked my permission. Mr. Key has barely arrived and I don't
have a clear judge of his abilities, although he comes highly
recommended from the person he was apprenticed to, William
Byers, and his uncle Peter Burford, whom I am sure you know."

"Yes, I know Burford, please have Mr. Key come in so
we can put this request to him." Wythe had a servant
fetch Key and put the proposition before him.

"Sir, I have barely begun to work for you," said Luck.
"However as you have not given me any major responsibilities
yet, I would be willing to take on this assignment if that
is your wish." Luck barely contained his enthusiasm.

"Sheriff Norvell has the right to request your assistance,"
said Wythe. "However, in this case, he has asked my
permission and I have agreed, if you are willing."

"Of course, sir," said Key. Luck thought that this would be
a fine opportunity for him to learn about the county and the
legal process. And it promised to be more interesting than
the copying work he would do as a junior clerk for Wythe.

Sheriff Norvell worked out the details with Wythe. He would
deputize Mr. Key and begin immediately to examine and
question persons who might have a further understanding of
the matter; first they would go out to the Johnson plantation.
Wythe volunteered to allow Luck to move his things into a
small room on the top floor of the Wythe house to use as his

temporary lodging and also, Wythe thought, so I can keep abreast of the investigation. Luck didn't have many "things," a change of clothes, a few mementos from his family, and a knife that his father gave him just before he died. "I can pick those up tomorrow when we are back from the plantation," said Key.

"The first necessity is to inform the family members of the death of Mr. Johnson," said Norvell. This was not a task that the Sheriff wanted to do, but there really was no one else he could delegate this task to. It would also give him a chance to talk to people at Johnson's plantation and try to see what they might know about possible reasons for such a clandestine meeting in the Powder Magazine on a Sunday night.

"We should have just enough time and light to ride to Johnson's plantation and inform the widow," said Norvell to Key.

Sheriff Norvell asked Mr. Wythe whether he would officially inform the House of Burgesses and the other representative from King William County, Carter Braxton. "Also, I am not aware of where Mr. Johnson stayed during the session of the House of Burgesses. Would you find out and with my authority examine his rooms for any evidence that might be relevant to the investigation." Wythe agreed to both requests.

CHAPTER 6

It was over twenty miles to Johnson's plantation, Rosebud, near the town of West Point, formed at the confluence of the Pamunkey and Mattaponi Rivers, which converge and become the York River, flowing into the Chesapeake Bay. Norvell thought they might make it there before dark but would have to stay overnight in the area before returning to Williamsburg.

Borrowing fresh horses from Wythe, they started out on the journey from Williamsburg to Johnson's plantation. Most of the road to the plantation was part of what people referred to as the King's Highway. The Highway was built under the orders of Charles II of England, who wanted to link all the colonies. In Virginia, the route begins in Suffolk at the North Carolina border and works its way along the coast up through Williamsburg, Stafford County, Fredericksburg, and Alexandria. So it was not surprising that they passed others going both ways—merchants with goods on their carts and an occasional rider. Sheriff Norvell knew a few of these individuals and said hello as they passed. Key and Norvell rode at a fairly good pace, alternating walking and trotting, just enough to feel the wind blowing through their hair, but not enough to unnecessarily tire out the horses before arriving at the plantation. They stopped twice at springs along the way to allow the horses to water and give the horses and riders a brief rest.

They talked a little about the case on the trip. It is possible,

thought Sheriff Norvell, that Mr. Johnson had been out walking
Sunday evening and seeing the Powder Magazine door open
went to investigate just as had Mr. Key, but whoever was there
surprised and silenced him. However, would James go into the
Magazine in the dark, even armed with a pistol? He would more
likely go with someone else, perhaps bringing a lantern, and
there was no evidence of a lantern in the Powder Magazine..

"I went in by myself," said Luck, "but of course it was light
and I did not need a lantern. I certainly would not have
investigated in the dark. Is it likely that Mr. Johnson did so?"

"I don't think so," said Norvell. "It seems more likely that
Mr. Johnson was there to meet someone. At that late hour,
I imagine that this was on some confidential matter. Why
it turned deadly is the question? And the reason for the
meeting is likely to give us the motive for the killing."

As they rode along the Kings Highway they passed through
some beautiful wooded areas, Red Cedars, Catalpas, and
the English Yew trees, along with the more common Oak
and Maple. They were all beginning to bud and leaf out,
their gentle light green hue enhanced by the afternoon
sun. To cross the Pamunkey River, and reach the site of
the Johnson Plantation, they made use of a ferry that was
in continual operation from dawn to dusk; they were
fortunate that they did not have to wait long. However,
it was nearly dark when they arrived at Rosebud. As they
approached the plantation manor house, a Negro butler
Samuel came out to greet them and ask their business.

"I am Sheriff Norvell of Williamsburg and James City County
and this is my deputy Mr. Key. Is your mistress available?"
asked the Sheriff. "And would you have someone care for
the horses? We have had a hard ride from Williamsburg."

"Yes, sir, I will have someone tend the horses and make sure
they are fed and wiped down after their long ride. Please come
into the parlor and I will inform Mrs. Johnson of your arrival."
The two men wiped the dust off of their clothes, scraped the
dirt off of their boots, as best they could, and entered the

house. The parlor was just to the right of the entrance.

After a short wait, Sarah Johnson came into the parlor. She was a lovely woman in her early 40s, still quite striking with dark brown hair and eyes. As was common in warmer weather, she had on a blue cotton dress over some number of petticoats. Her hair was mostly tucked under a lace cap and she wore a silk kerchief around her neck.

Because she had never met the two men, she was naturally curious and worried about what news they might bring. "Why would they be here this late in the evening?" she thought.

Sheriff Norvell and Mr. Key stood and the Sheriff introduced himself and his deputy. Luck was visibly nervous as he was unfamiliar with how to speak of these terrible events— and was glad that Norvell took the lead. There is no way to render bad news gracefully and Sheriff Norvel immediately explained why they were there. "I am sorry to inform you that your husband is dead. We are very sorry for your loss."

"What happened?" asked Mrs. Johnson, clearly stunned by the news. She grabbed hold of a chair for support. "Are you sure that this is true? He was in good health when he left for Williamsburg."

"Unfortunately, I am sure," said Sheriff Norvell. "I am familiar with your husband and his identity was confirmed by George Wythe, whom I expect you know. I also have to tell you that his was not a natural death. He was murdered sometime late Sunday night or early this morning."

"Murdered! I cannot believe it." Mrs. Johnson face turned ashen and she started to faint. Norvell caught her and called for Samuel to help her into a seat in a sofa by the fireplace, though as it was warm the fire was not lit.

"Is there someone you can summon to help your mistress?" asked Norvell.

Samuel went to find Mrs. Johnson's daughter Bethany and she came downstairs and asked what the problem was. When told, she too was visibly shocked about the sudden news, but for a young women she was composed and ministered to her mother

as best she could. Both women were sobbing and the two men
were very uncomfortable and sorry to be the cause of such grief.

"We do not want to further impose on you tonight,"
said Sheriff Norvell. "But we would like to return
tomorrow morning and discuss this further with
you and your plantation staff. The inquest will be
on Thursday afternoon in Williamsburg."

Recovering somewhat, Mrs. Johnson asked the men if
they would like to stay the night. "It is no trouble, we have
guest rooms that could easily be made up for you."

While tempting, Sheriff Norvell thought that he did not
want to impose on them tonight and he wanted to have a
chance to talk to Key before coming back in the morning.
"That is most generous of you," said Norvell, "but we
have made other arrangements for tonight." The two men
took their leave, retrieved their horses, and headed into
town to find a tavern for supper and a place to sleep.

✻　✻　✻

That same night George Wythe dined with the Lieutenant
Governor. This was an occasional occurrence and Wythe
was not surprised to get the invitation, even though it came
late in the afternoon. He liked Governor Francis Fauquier
and had enjoyed many pleasant evenings of discussions with
him, often joined by Professor William Small of the College
of William and Mary and more recently Thomas Jefferson.
But tonight he thought it would be just the two of them.

As was true in most of the colonies, Fauquier was a
"substitute" governor. Many governors were appointed
with the idea of receiving some income and prestige but
did not want to relocate from 'cultured' England to the
wilds of the colonies. Fauquier was appointed lieutenant
governor in 1758 by Governor John Campbell, the 4th Earl

of Loudon, and when Campbell was succeeded by Jeffery Amherst as governor, Amherst kept Fauquier in his role as lieutenant governor. Lieutenant governors exercised all of the duties of a governor, were referred to as the Governor, and lived in the Royal Governor's Palace at the end of the Palace Green, just a few steps from Wythe's home. His financial remuneration was modest but sufficient for him to entertain and live well in the Governor's Palace.

There is always gossip that accompanies any Royal appointment. Fauquier was thought to be deeply in debt because of excessive gambling. Through the intervention of friends, Fauquier was spared embarrassment through this appointment, allowing him to get out of town and out of the way of his creditors. It was rumored that Lord George Anson, previously the First Lord of the Admiralty, was one on the people Fauquier had lost large sums to. However in an act of beneficence, Lord Anson advocated for Fauquier to be appointed lieutenant-governor of Virginia.

George Wythe liked Fauquier, though he was unhappy that he had introduced heavy gambling into the upper societies of Virginia. But Governor Fauquier was cultured and charming with an intellectual side that went further than many local aristocratic gentlemen or past governors of Virginia. He was a fellow of the Royal Society of London and wrote a well-regarded monograph about how to raise money without increasing public debt. He suggested rather than a consumer tax, there should be a graduated income tax on higher incomes—an enlightened view thought Wythe. He also pleaded for better treatment of Native-American Indians. Unfortunately, neither of his ideas received a warm welcome in Parliament, though Wythe felt both ideas had merit.

The Royal Governor's Palace was an impressive building; Wythe thought one of the most important in Virginia and it exuded the power of the Crown. Gilded iron gates at the entrance to the brick walled grounds were flanked by the symbols of a lion, a unicorn and crowns of England. The Palace was a three-story Baroque style building topped with a two-story tower. The public rooms were mostly downstairs, with the family quarters on the second floor. The Governor also kept a well-stocked cellar that could store 6,000 bottles of wine.

Although the night was heavy with humidity, Wythe would have enjoyed walking the grounds of the Palace as several acres of terraced gardens were available to guests of the Governor and open for occasional events. He and Elizabeth had done so many times. As he walked through the gates he could smell meat roasting on the spits in the kitchen that was to the left of the Palace. Looking to his right he saw the Palace stables for the governor's horses and Royal carriage.

Wythe had dressed appropriately in a single-breasted black broadcloth coat and a long vest, with large pocket-flaps and a strait collar, but it was less formal than many who would be invited to the Palace. He wore his long brown hair tied up behind him rather than wearing a wig, which he wore only on very special occasions.

Mr. Wythe was welcomed by George, the governor's butler. They knew each other well and exchanged greetings. Before going up the stairs, Wythe stopped to look at the large round foyer, decorated with sabers, pistols, pikes and muskets. It was meant to be a bit intimidating—and it was, although by now Wythe was used to it. The rooms of the Palace were covered by walnut paneling, with marble fireplaces, and inlaid floors. A beautiful pine staircase led to the upper level of the Palace. He had been to the Palace many times and he and his wife enjoyed the large ballroom just off the foyer, which was used for a variety of entertaining, music and dancing, enabling the ladies of Virginia and visitors to display the latest fashions from England and France.

He met the Governor in the upstairs public "middle room," used by the Governor for his official business and meetings with Virginia officials. The other upstairs rooms consisted of the personal rooms of the family. The Governor had a surprise guest, their neighbor Robert Carter III, a wealthy plantation owner and member of the Virginia Royal Council or Governor's Council as it was referred to. Carter was largely self-educated, as Wythe, but had the opportunity of studying at London's Inns of Court before coming back to Virginia. He was a member of the Virginia Bar and one of the few persons who shared Wythe's views on the evils of slavery. His house was on the same side of the Palace Green as Wythe's and a bit closer to the Palace.

Since it was just the three of them for supper, Governor Fauquier suggested that they eat in this room rather in the official dining room downstairs. Wythe enjoyed the room, which was a bit smaller than the formal parlor downstairs. He thought it comfortable but not too informal. The Governor maintained a considerable library at one end of the room, and he and Wythe often exchanged books that the other person might have an interest in. There was a small table in the center of the room, with four side chairs and a sofa and arm chairs along the wall opposite the library books. So the room could fulfill a variety of official or private functions. The room had an iron furnace in addition to the fireplace for colder nights, although the weather, despite the humidity, was quite nice. They were able to leave the windows open towards the gardens below where they felt the breezes coming from the northwest, gently blowing and cooling the room.

The Governor dressed casually, he did not need to demonstrate his status through his clothes—a quality that Wythe liked. Robert Carter was dressed a bit more formally, with a flowing silk great coat, but he too kept his brown hair tied behind him and did not wear a wig that he might have worn on more official occasions.

The servants had set out a delicious looking buffet of cold fish and meats, cheeses and breads for the gentlemen. They ate off of Royal chinaware, designed for the Governor, and used silver utensils that he had brought from England. The food included smoked bacon, fish from the nearby James River, and both domestic and foreign cheeses that had just come off the ship *Hope*, which just landed from

England that day. A variety of wines was available; they started out with a nice German Riesling with the fish and then had a hardier French Burgundy with the meat dishes. George was the only server and he made sure their wine glasses were full and empty plates taken promptly away.

After enjoying the supper and engaging in light news and discussions about family, the early warm weather, and a status on the Johnson murder investigation, Wythe and Carter accepted a glass of brandy and Wythe asked the Governor about what information he had received from England.

"That is the reason for the short notice for supper tonight," Fauquier replied. "And I have some bad news that I wanted to share with you before officially informing the House of Burgesses and Governor's Council. Despite the protests of Virginia and other colonies, Parliament has enacted the Stamp Act. A letter I received from a cousin indicated that the action was done with little debate and no consideration of the position of the colonies."

"I'm worried about what actions the news might trigger. So far Virginia has been relatively constrained in comparison to Massachusetts, whose legislature has been at odds with Parliament over a number of measures. I would hate to see marches and other mischief here in Virginia, even though you know I am in sympathy with your position."

Wythe was shaken by the news. "I guess I should have expected it, but to not even consider the petitions of the colonies, including our own from our Committee on Correspondence, is extremely disheartening. I can't tell you how the House of Burgesses will react to the news, but I would not be surprised at some type of protest. They know that you did not support the Act, so no one will hold you personally to blame. Though as a representative of the Crown, you are likely to bear the brunt of the criticism."

Carter echoed Wythe's thoughts. He said that he personally was not offended by the Stamp Act, but was worried about the precedent of Parliament enacting laws without discussion

and input from the House of Burgesses and the Governor's
Council. "I'm afraid this will put us at odds with Parliament,"
said Carter, "undoubtedly we will want to establish a
clear position in opposition to Parliament's actions."

"I would recommend that you listen and not respond
sharply. Assume that calmer heads in the House of
Burgesses will eventually prevail," said Wythe. "Although
I wish I could feel the same about Parliament. But they
do not seem interested in finding a middle ground."

They said goodnight to the Governor and walked out
together to return to their respective homes, much troubled
by the news from England and wondering what might occur
in the future. "Will we remain loyal to Great Britain or work
to end this long relationship, which both England and the
colonies have benefited from?" Wythe asked himself.

❈ ❈ ❈

Sheriff Norvell and Key had supper at the Black Horse
Tavern in West Point that night after leaving the Johnson's
plantation. It had been a long day and both were tired and
hungry. It was late so the tavern was not busy. They had grilled
crabs from the Chesapeake Bay, cold roast pork, bread and
a fruit torte for desert. After their initial hunger and thirst
were satiated, Norvell asked Luck about his background
and how he came to be George Wythe's junior clerk.

"My father was Martin Key, the son of the Martin Key Sr., and
grandson of John Key. John and Martin Sr. came to Virginia in
1688 from East Riding, Yorkshire, England." said Luck. "I do
not know why they chose to immigrate to Virginia. I have
heard they were caught up in the religious conflict going on in
England at the time, when James II was overthrown in favor of
his daughter Mary. There was fear that James II and the heir were
Papist and would turn the country back from its protestant

35

faith toward Rome. And of course there were promises of land
and more freedom in Virginia. There was a great population
growth in England at the time and only so much land; Virginia
must have seemed like the Promised Land to them."

"My father married Elizabeth Burford, granddaughter of
William Burford, who had immigrated in the mid-1600s
from Oxfordshire, England. Unfortunately, both of my
parents died before I was of age, so I was apprenticed
briefly to plantation owner William Byers."

"How did you come to be called Luck?" Norvell asked.

"Well I have been told that my mother's pregnancy was
difficult and I was lucky to be born, so that might be the reason"
said Luck, who also noted that he had a slight limp because
of the birth difficulties. "But I am also aware that there was
another family with the last name of Luck in neighboring
Albermarle County so perhaps that was the real reason. I am
always kidded about my name. I don't feel particularly lucky
or unlucky. You have to make use of your opportunities in
this world and not expect luck to play a major role in your
life. Though I feel fortunate that I was taken on by Mr. Wythe,
a man everyone respects. I just asked him at the estate closing
if a clerk position was available and he agreed to give me a
chance. My father always used to tell me that you made your
own luck in the world and to not rely on your name."

"That certainly is a good attitude and good advice,"
said Norvell. "My family is descended from a Scottish
line that goes back to the earliest colonial settlers in the
1600s. My grandfather, Capt. Hugh Norvell, fought in the
wars against the French and Indians, and I served under
him, picking up some useful military knowledge. Capt.
Norvell was an important vestryman at Burton Church,
and now I hold that position. The old Scottish adage is to
work hard and you will succeed, and most of us did."

As they finished up their after dinner brandy, the Sheriff asked
Mr. Key what his first observations were of the investigation.

"Well," said Luck, "I can't imagine anyone in the

family having a responsibility for Mr. Johnson's death.
They obviously were stunned by the news. Mrs.
Johnson seemed shocked as did her daughter."
Norvell said he shared that conclusion.

"Bethany certainly was a beautiful young woman.
How old do you think she is?" asked Luck.

"I expect that she is in her mid-teens," said Sheriff Norvell.
"I agree that she is quite attractive and she reminds me
of my own daughter Johanna, now in England. Don't get
any ideas about her. I am sure her parents hoped to marry
her to a large plantation owner so that they might benefit
from the marriage. Now of course her prospects must be
somewhat reduced, and she will need to take care of her
mother with her father now dead. Let's try to get some
sleep. We will have a busy and long day again tomorrow."

CHAPTER 7

Tuesday May 21

George Wythe thought about the strange happenings of the previous day as he went to find his fellow member of the House of Burgesses, Carter Braxton, who like James Johnson was from King William County. There was a lot riding on how this investigation was handled. Mr. Johnson was a respected member of the House of Burgesses and if the murder was reaction to some political position Johnson took, Wythe was worried about the potential political fallout. Mr. Johnson was usually aligned with the more conservative plantation representatives but Wythe could not imagine a political motive for the murder. In any case, finding the perpetrator was the first priority. Wythe also had to let Braxton know about the Stamp Act, although he expected the Governor would send a message to the House of Burgesses today about the matter.

Wythe thought that Sheriff William Norvell was a good man and up for the challenge of investigating the murder. He was not deeply learned, but had a solid mind. He was even tempered and most people respected him, even though he had the unenviable task of collecting taxes owed. He was fair and would make every attempt to find a way for debtors to pay the required amount without enduring unnecessary punishment. When all things were considered, Wythe doubted that there were few others in the community better able to take charge of the investigation.

Wythe's new junior clerk, Luck Key, was a bit of an enigma. He was a gangly youth, a bit under 6 feet tall, with strong features and piercing blue-gray eyes. He did seem bright, with the kind of curiosity that probably provided an additional advantage in assisting Norvell. Wythe had barely offered Mr. Key his clerk position, when he was co-opted by Norvell. It was hard to blame the young man for his obvious excitement. Certainly participating in a murder investigation was a lot more interesting than the mundane chores of a junior clerk.

Wythe thought about his upcoming meeting. Carter Braxton, the grandson of Robert "King" Carter, was one of the wealthiest and most powerful landowners in Virginia. Educated at the College of William and Mary, Braxton had served King William County in a variety of political and community positions and was briefly the sheriff of the county and now its representative in the House of Burgesses. Braxton maintained a substantial plantation and in Virginia politics he generally was allied with Landon Carter, Edmund Randolph and other conservative planters.

He found Braxton at the Raleigh Tavern having breakfast and asked if he could have a few minutes of his time. He let Braxton know that it was important and though asked as a request, Braxton understood the imperative and asked Wythe to join him for coffee. Although he had already consumed his light breakfast of porridge, bread and coffee, the breakfast coffee at the Raleigh Tavern was too good to pass up and Wythe sat down and joined Braxton.

"I am afraid I have some sad and shocking, news," Wythe told Braxton. "Your colleague James Johnson was murdered Sunday night or sometime early Monday morning. The Sheriff has been informed and is notifying the family. He asked me to tell you so that you might tell others who need to know as well as officially inform the House of Burgesses tomorrow."

Braxton seemed stunned by the news and slumped into his chair. "How did this happen?" he asked. "Who is responsible? Poor Sarah! She must be devastated. I must immediately send a messenger to inform my wife so that she can provide whatever assistance is necessary. Our plantations are relatively close to one another."

"What I can tell you," said Wythe, "is that James Johnson was likely meeting someone in the Powder Magazine late at night when he was viciously attacked from behind and killed. Now it will be up to the Sheriff to determine why and who is responsible. The inquest will be Thursday afternoon."

"The Powder Magazine? That doesn't make any sense. Why would he meet someone there?" Braxton asked.

"That is the main mystery of course," said Wythe. "If we knew why he was meeting someone, it would give us an insight into who might have done this murder. Was there anything going on in Johnson's life that was strange or might lead to such an act? Were there any personal issues in his life that might lead someone to seek revenge? Or difficult business dealings that might have created an enemy?"

"Of course not!" Braxton immediately reacted. Then he thought some more. "I do know that like many planters, James was in some financial difficulty, given the drop in the price of tobacco. I suppose this could have been about money. But why would you kill someone who owed you money? You would have no hope of repayment. So that doesn't make sense."

"James was not known as a philanderer, and he had a good reputation in terms of his business dealings, so I don't see revenge as a likely motive. In fact, I can't think of any motive for someone killing him. I will of course provide the official notification to the House of Burgesses," said Braxton. "Thank you for informing me first. This is bad business. I hope Sheriff Norvell is up to the task of solving this mystery."

"I am confident in his abilities," said Wythe, "but we may yet uncover a political motivation of some sort for the crime and that may be something we or other members of the House of Burgesses will have to deal with. I respect Norvell, but he does not have the political power that you

and some other members do and any accusations against
a member of the House would be extremely sensitive."

"Sheriff Norvell also asked me to check out Mr. Johnson's
lodgings. Do you know where he usually stayed?' asked Wythe.

"I believe he usually lived in the same boarding house on
Nassau Street as John Page," said Braxton. "I think it is run by
a Mrs. George, though I am not sure of that. James and John
enjoyed one another's company, liked the food served there,
and it was away from the noise of the Duke of Gloucester
Street, but not too far from the Capitol Building,"

"Thank you, I know Mrs. George's lodging. One other matter,"
said Wythe. "Governor Fauquier informed me last night that
he had official news from England that the Stamp Act had
passed Parliament, apparently with little consideration of
the petitions of our Committee on Correspondence or of the
views of the other colonies. I am apprehensive about the
next steps and how the House of Burgesses should react."

"I don't like it any more than you," said Braxton. "I
know it is the principle more than the money involved,
still it is not a lot of money. I wonder whether it makes
sense to continue to protest it. I just don't know."

"Nor I," replied Wythe, "I will see you at the next session,
if not before, and we can speak about this further."

Wythe walked west on the Duke of Gloucester Street
toward the College of William and Mary and turned south on
Nassau Street going a few blocks until he came to the George
guest house. Its owner Julia George answered the door, when
Wythe knocked, and greeted him. "Mr. George Wythe it is
good to see you again, it has been awhile since you handled
the legal matters regarding the purchase of this guest house.
It has saved me financially and I am continually grateful
for your assistance. What brings you here?" she asked.

"Sad news, I am afraid," said Wythe. "I understand
that House of Burgesses representative James
Johnson stayed with you during the session."

"Yes," she said, "but I have not seen him today and it

does not look like he slept in his room last night."

"I'm afraid Mr. Johnson was murdered Sunday night or early Monday morning," said Wythe. "Sheriff Norvell has asked me to go through his room for possible evidence and to speak to John Page, if he is here."

Mrs. George was thunderstruck. "I can't believe this. Please come in and tell me what you know."

"I'm afraid I am not allowed to tell you too much. There will be an inquest Thursday afternoon. But I can tell you that he must have met someone at the Powder Magazine and was murdered there. Is Mr. Page here?" asked Wythe.

"No, he indicated that he had business elsewhere and left last Sunday, I believe, and has not been back since then, though I do expect him back before the next meeting of the House of Burgesses. Let me show you Mr. Johnson's room," said Mrs. George.

Wythe went with her and examined the small room that Mr. Johnson used while in Williamsburg, it adjoined the room that Mr. Page occupied while in Williamsburg. It was nicely but minimally furnished: a single bed, nightstand, and small armoire that held Johnson's clothes. Wythe quickly went through the items in the room and could uncover no notes or anything else that might lead them to discover who he was meeting with at the Magazine.

He thanked Mrs. George and asked her to inform Mr. Page of Johnson's death when he returned and to ask Page to get in touch with the Sheriff or Wythe as soon as possible. Julia indicated that she would do so and encouraged Mr. Wythe to stop by her home with Elizabeth sometime in the future.

"We would enjoy that," said Wythe.

CHAPTER 8

After a quick breakfast porridge of cornmeal and oats and buttered bread at the Black Horse Tavern, Sheriff William Norvell and his deputy Luck Key were back on their horses, headed to the Johnson Plantation. Key had managed little sleep as his roommate for the night, the Sheriff, was a heavy snorer and flatulent from the large supper last night. Still, Luck was excited to be working with Norvell.

Arriving at the Johnson Plantation, they were met again by Samuel, the Negro butler, who took charge of the horses and invited them to rest in the parlor or front room, where they were shortly joined by Sarah Johnson and her daughter Bethany. Mrs. Johnson obviously had been crying and had deep circles under her eyes, but she was reasonably composed given the dreadful situation. She was now more formally dressed in black polonaise gown, with buttons up the front, a black cap and little jewelry other than a strand of pearls she wore around her neck.

Sheriff Norvell thought she was lovely in the simplicity and elegance of her dress. He again expressed sorrow and sympathy for her loss and asked if she would be able to answer a few questions. She agreed. "When was the last time you saw your husband?" asked Norvell.

"He was here ten days ago, during a break in the House of Burgesses meetings," responded Mrs. Johnson. "He said he would not be back this past weekend as he had business to attend to, but would see me this coming Friday or Saturday."

"Do you know what business kept Mr. Johnson in Williamsburg over last weekend?" asked Norvell. "We are trying to discover his movements and who he may have met with. Anything you can tell us would be greatly helpful."

"Sheriff, you can appreciate that my husband kept the business of managing the plantation largely to himself. I was responsible for the running the household and everyday expenses, but knew very little about the operations of the plantation. You might find out more by asking the overseer, John Mechem."

"Was he worried about anything in particular? Or did he mention anyone that he had concerns about?" continued the Sheriff.

"Well, of course he was worried about the price of tobacco and its effect on the plantation operations. But I really cannot recall anyone that he mentioned that he was concerned about. Certainly, no one that would want to kill him. Could this have been a mistake?" asked Mrs. Johnson.

"While that is always a possibility," stated Norvell, "it seems unlikely in this situation. It certainly appears like your husband went to the Powder Magazine to meet someone and whoever that person was killed him. May we look at the plantation accounts, there may be some information that could assist us. We will of course keep all of the financial details confidential, unless it is essential to the investigation."

"Yes, of course, if you think it will assist you." said Mrs. Johnson. "I will ask Mr. Mechem to meet with you in my husband's library and he can probably answer questions about the accounts and plantation operations better than I."

"Two last questions, Mrs. Johnson," said Norvell. "Would your husband have been carrying anything of value on him or documents of any kind? And did he own a pistol?"

"I am not aware that my husband was carrying anything of value," said Mrs. Johnson. "He seldom carried much cash with him and other than his wedding ring he would not likely have had anything of great value on his person. He did own a small pistol and often had it with

him. I am sorry I could not be more helpful." She began
to cry, thinking of her husband's untimely death.

"Thank you very much Mrs. Johnson," said Norvell. "You
have been very forthright and helpful given the difficult
situation. Is there anything that we can do to assist you?
The inquest will be Thursday afternoon at 4 pm. You are
not obliged to attend but are welcome to do so."

"Thank you, but I am not sure I am able to bear the
strain," said Mrs. Johnson. "Carter Braxton's plantation is
near us and I asked one of my servant to ride over there
last night and inform his wife about what has happened.
Mrs. Braxton sent me word that she will come over today
to provide me assistance, so I think I will be all right.
Though I can't imagine a future without my husband."

A short while later, they were waiting to meet with Mr.
Mechem in the Johnson library. The library was typical of a
southern plantation house. There was a wall of bookshelves
with a number of books that likely were handed down
in the family or procured from England and a wood desk,
which contained the plantation records. Two paintings,
perhaps of Johnson's parents, were hanging on one of
the walls. The servants brought refreshments, water,
whiskey, and some small cakes that were very tasty.

When John Mechem joined Key and Norvell in the Library,
Luck observed that he was not the most pleasant looking
person, though he knew not to judge someone by their looks.
He expected Mechem was also distressed about losing Mr.
Johnson and wondering about his future. Still, Luck thought
he was not as gracious as he might considering the situation.
Sheriff Norvell, however, seemed to ignore Mr. Mechem's
uncivil attitude and began to review the plantation books with
him. Key continued to take notes of Mechem's comments as
he had done earlier during the questioning of Mrs. Johnson.

"As you can see," stated Mechem, "the plantation is land
rich and cash poor, like many in Virginia. I would not say
the debt was overwhelming, but some of the creditors

have been pushing for payment and there were concerns
over obtaining additional credit. I know Mr. Johnson had
been considering selling some of his land holdings. And
we did have to sell five slaves last year to balance the cash
needs. He did not want to do that, but really did not have
any choice. When last I saw Mr. Johnson, he seemed more
optimistic. He told me that he believed he had found a
way to meet his short-term credit needs and was hoping
to conclude those negotiations in Williamsburg."

"Did he tell you with whom he was
negotiating," asked Norvell.

"No, he was a bit secretive about it, but I just assumed that
since he did not have the deal concluded, he preferred not to
identify the persons he was meeting with" stated Mechem.
"I just can't imagine who would have wanted him dead.
He was well liked and as far as I know had no enemies."

Thinking some more about the situation, Mechem
volunteered, "There was some trouble when we sold
the five slaves last year. One of the Negroes, Jacob, was
our general carpenter and blacksmith. He was well-
regarded and valuable so it made some sense to sell Jacob
as he could get a good price. Mr. Johnson did sell him to
James Anderson, the Williamsburg blacksmith, as Mr.
Anderson's business was expanding because of his increased
commissions on behalf of the Governor and others."

"What then was the trouble about?" asked Norvell.

"Unfortunately we were not able to keep Jacob together
with his wife and children," said Mechem, "and they were
sold off to another plantation owner. This was not something
Mr. Johnson wanted to do; he always tried to keep families
together. But these are difficult times. Jacob and his family were
all very upset as you can imagine. There was a lot of crying
and some words were said. Jacob has a bit of temper and I had
to occasionally discipline him. Since he is with Mr. Anderson
in Williamsburg, you should check that out. It seems almost
unimaginable that Jacob would strike down his old master, but

he did have a temper and I guess there was some bad blood."

"Thank you for that piece of information. We will surely investigate that possibility," Norvell responded. "I would like you to attend the inquest on Thursday afternoon at four in case questions arise that you could answer. It is too much for Mrs. Johnson to attend and I think someone should represent the family."

Sheriff Norvell and Key took their leave of Mr. Mechem and Mrs. Johnson and after having dinner at the tavern where they had previously stayed they began the long ride back to Williamsburg. Both were mostly quiet on the return trip, as they thought over what they had learned and what they did and didn't know.

Luck asked the Sheriff what he thought of Mr. Mechem. "Well, he is not the most pleasant person in the world, but overseers are not noted for their likeability. They often don't stay long in one place, but often move to try to make enough money for their own farm. Mr. Mechem is tall and looked strong. Certainly he would have been capable of dealing Mr. Johnson a murderous blow with a halberd, but I can't see a motive for him doing so," replied the Sheriff, "unless there was some financial mismanagement that Mechem is concealing."

On the way back they decided to stop at the Wythe house and see if they could arrange a meeting with Mr. Wythe. It was supper time and Wythe invited them to join him for some food and drink. He recounted his meeting with Carter Braxton, his search of Johnson's room, and the fact that Mr. Johnson's friend and fellow Burgesses John Page was out of town. In turn Norvell and Key described their discussions at the Johnson plantation.

"What I can't understand," said Key, "is the financial structure of plantations like the Johnson's. It seems like he was in a great deal of debt and almost constantly so. Yet he was regarded as a wealthy plantation owner. It doesn't make sense to me." Both Wythe and Norvell looked at him. Key's father had not been a plantation owner so Luck would not understand the nature of Virginia plantations.

"Let me try to provide an overview of plantation operations," said Wythe. "I own a small plantation near Elizabeth City. An overseer runs the plantation and takes care of the books. While I have a modest manor house there, I don't staff it full-time. When I go there, I take my servants from here rather than pay for a duplicate set of servants to live there. Even so, the plantation barely breaks even on a good year and were it not for my legal fees as a practitioner of law I would constantly worry about debt."

"The same is true for me," said Sheriff Norvell. "The real problem is that plantations are very labor intensive and short on capital. Plantation operations require many acres of land to justify the money spent on production: the land, seed, Negroes, the feeding and caring of the laborers and other expenses. All of this requires money, which is typically borrowed from sources in England or Scotland and paid back with the products produced in Virginia—primarily tobacco." "The other critical factor is the British sterling exchange rate, which has recently risen to the highest point that anyone can remember. Thus it takes more tobacco to pay back the debts. And if the price of tobacco falls because of surplus or reduced demand it really creates more pressure on the plantation owners," said Norvell.

"Of course as you buy more land and slaves," said Wythe, "you are expected to maintain a large manor house that welcomes visitors and holds parties. You also are supposed to provide leadership for the community. All of that requires even more money, which places an additional financial burden on the plantation owner. The production and expenditures do provide a financial base for the tradespeople living in the towns, so while they may not be directly benefiting from the tobacco sales plantations create an economy that sustains thousands of people in Virginia."

"But couldn't the plantation owners live a bit more modestly?" asked Luck. "Wouldn't this put less pressure on the owners to have to borrow more money?"

Norvell and Wythe shrugged their shoulders as if this was
not a real option. "I think plantation owners are optimistic
about the future and because of that are willing to borrow
more. It is only when we have a big drop in prices or an
increase in the sterling exchange rate, as recently occurred,
that owners really feel the pinch," concluded Wythe.

Sheriff Norvell excused himself, saying he was going to
try to set up meetings with Carter Braxton and some other
members of the House of Burgesses in the morning. He said
he would stop by in the morning about eight for Mr. Key
and that they would conduct another round of interviews.
He thanked Mr. Wythe for his hospitality and left.

George Wythe asked Luck how he enjoyed working with
Norvell and what he thought about the investigation so far.
"I like working with the Sheriff," said Key. "He is thoughtful
and listens well and handled the interview with Mrs. Johnson
with a great deal of grace. I really don't know what to make
of the investigation at this point. Mr. Johnson appears
to have no enemies. He seemed devoted to his wife and
daughter and no one seems to have any idea who murdered
him. There was some trouble over a Negro who was sold to
blacksmith James Anderson, while his family was sold to
another plantation owner. So a revenge murder is possible."

"Still, I think the financial issue is the one that may lead us
somewhere. Mr. Johnson was in debt. He was trying to negotiate
some relief from someone. That seems to be the crux. But I
honestly don't know where to go from here," concluded Key.
"Hopefully the Sheriff will have some ideas before the inquest."

Wythe nodded. "You are probably right. You have had
a long two days. Try to get some rest. I have to look over
some files and do not need you for the rest of the day."

Luck rose and as he went up the steps to the second floor he
met George's wife Elizabeth. She asked how he was doing in
this strange new position and whether he needed anything
for his small room. Luck was used to sharing a room with
someone and said "It is a very nice room and I am thankful

you and Mr. Wythe have provided it for me. It is really a
luxury to have your own room. When I was growing up
I always shared a room with at least two of my brothers.
As an apprentice I shared rooms with others, including
two indentured servants that worked for Mr. Byers."

"Well I am sure it is nice to share a room and have someone
to talk to," said Mrs. Wythe, "but as you are now eighteen
I expect you like to have a room for yourself. It was not
really designed as a bedroom, but I hope you will be happy
here while working for George. He has taken a liking to
you and I am glad you are here to assist him. You will be
able to save money from paying lodging expenses that will
help you with your own career when the time is right."

"Thank you Ma'am," said Luck. "I appreciate that very much
and wish you a good night." Luck thought that Elizabeth
Wythe was one of the most charming and kind persons
that he had met, reminding him of a refined and gentrified
version of his own mother who also was named Elizabeth.

Elizabeth entered the bedroom that she shared with her
husband George. Sometimes he would work into the late night
in his law office downstairs, but he usually came up to share
the events of the day and what he was thinking about. She
did not have his education, but he had taught her the love of
learning and she always read in the evening before going to
sleep. Often George would ask her what she thought about a
certain situation and sometimes she believed she was a bit
more practical than George, which perhaps is why they were
such a compatible couple. They had their ups and downs.
Married at only fifteen, she had no idea what was expected of a
wife, let alone the wife of someone with increasing influence
in Williamsburg. They had lost their first child and with great
sadness had learned that she could bear no more children.

George had been saddened but did not blame Elizabeth. It
was God's will, he said. Perhaps that is why he enjoyed having
young people around like Tom Jefferson and Luck Key. They
often were surrogate sons. And he just liked people, liked to

teach them, liked to debate the issues of the day with them and enjoyed their successes as he would have had he had a son. While not the same, she too liked to assist the young men who apprenticed with George. She didn't try to mother or smother them, but did mention or make suggestions when she thought it would aid them in their own development.

She tried to anticipate George's needs and see to them in a simple manner. He reciprocated and was always solicitous of her. When she wanted to do something, go to a ball or take a trip to a friend of theirs outside of Williamsburg, George was almost always accommodating.

CHAPTER 9

Wednesday May 22

Wednesday was cloudy and gray, reflecting Norvell's own mood about the Johnson case. He stopped by the Wythe house to pick up Mr. Key and the two of them walked down to the house where House of Burgesses Speaker John Robinson was staying while in Williamsburg. Even though Braxton would have informed the Speaker of James Johnson's death, Norvell hoped the Speaker might provide some insights into Johnson's possible thinking and motives for meeting someone at the Powder Magazine.

Norvell told Key that John Robinson was considered the head of one of the "first families of Virginia," families who were both socially prominent and wealthy. They descended from early English colonists who primarily settled in Jamestown, Williamsburg, the Northern Neck of Virginia, along the James River and other navigable waters in Virginia. The Robinson plantation was Hedwick Manor in Middlesex, but he stayed in Williamsburg during the sessions of the House of Burgesses and for the social season. Typically these 'first families' generally married within their social class and often were among the more conservative of the plantation owners.

Robinson had been Speaker of the House of Burgesses since 1738 and was considered a fixture in that positon. He also held the position of Treasurer of the Colony and taxes that Norvell collected were put into the Treasury by Robinson. Obviously, thought Luck, Robinson was a person of great importance and wealth. Robinson's butler Henry opened the door and recognized Sheriff Norvell. He showed the two gentlemen into the house and to the parlor, where Robinson typically entertained guests. He settled them in, asked if they wanted any refreshments, and went to find his master. Speaker Robinson appeared after a short wait.

"What can I do for you two gentlemen," asked Robinson, who knew Norvell and was introduced to Mr. Key, his deputy.

"We are investigating the death of James Johnson," said Norvell.

"Yes, I supposed that was your purpose," said Robinson. "Of course his death came as a great shock to me and my colleagues when Carter Braxton told us the news yesterday. I don't believe I have any information that would be useful to your inquiry but I am happy to answer any questions you might have."

"When Mr. Key and I went over James Johnson's finances with his overseer John Mechem," said Norvell, "we were struck by the fact that Mr. Johnson was in serious debt. The overseer mentioned that he might have to sell-off some of his land and last year he sold some of his slaves to keep his creditors from pressing action."

"Well I know that many plantation owners are cash poor," said Robinson. "I had not realized that Mr. Johnson was in such dire straits."

"Did he come to you to borrow funds?" asked Norvell.

"No." said Robinson. "Of course I would have been glad to consider helping him if possible, but there are limits to what I could do and I have my own financial issues to deal with."

They informed Speaker Robinson that the inquest would be held at the Courthouse at 4 pm Thursday. He stated that he would not be present as he had other business and wished them well in their investigation. Thanking the Speaker, Norvell and Key left a few minutes later.

A short walk took them to the blacksmith shop. They found James Anderson at his forge finishing an ax, one of the necessities for clearing property and chopping wood for heat. Anderson's forge consisted of a raised brick hearth, with bellows to keep the coal fire hot, and a hood to carry away the smoke. The forge heated iron until it was malleable so that the blacksmith and his journeymen and apprentices could shape the iron into various items they made. Sledges weighing up to twelve pounds were used to hammer the iron into axes, special hammers, brackets and hinges, and a variety of business related and household necessities.

Mr. Anderson and his workers were all sweating as it was very warm in the shop and the slight breeze did not alleviate the heat. Among the workers was a large Negro, who they assumed was Jacob. He certainly would have been strong enough to deal the fatal blow to Mr. Johnson. Mr. Anderson turned over his work to one of the other men and went over to Norvell. "What can I do for you Sheriff? I hope you are not after me for back taxes, William. I think I am current with my payments."

"I am glad you are current, James. No it is not taxes that are our concern today; we came to talk to you about Jacob," said Norvell. "I understand you bought Jacob from James Johnson late last year, and that perhaps Jacob was not very pleased to be separated from his family. You know that Mr. Johnson was killed late Sunday night or early Monday morning."

"Yes, I heard about the murder. Jacob was very upset about his separation from his wife and children and he was very moody and uncooperative when I first brought him here," said Anderson. "However, Jacob has excellent skills that are important to the blacksmith shop. He also came so highly recommended that I made a deal with him. If he works hard for me for seven years, I will free him and then perhaps he could earn enough money to buy his family's freedom."

"I know that freeing slaves is not common but I wanted his best work and seven years of his service will provide

a fair return for my money. I also told him I would allow
him to visit his wife and children every other Sunday," said
Anderson. "In fact this past Sunday was one of his visiting
days. I allow him to borrow a horse and I always provide him
with a note so that he is not suspected of being a runaway."

"So to the best of your knowledge he was gone on Sunday,"
asked Norvell. "When does he usually return?"

"He must return by midnight," said Anderson. "That is part
of our agreement, and he has always done that. I didn't check
last Sunday, but I have no doubt that he made it back by that
time. He was up early and ready to work for me on Monday."

"Could we talk to Jacob?" Norvell asked.

"Of course," replied Anderson and he called over Jacob.
"Jacob, after your visit with your family on Sunday,
did you return by midnight?" asked Norvell.

"Yes sir," said Jacob. "I am grateful that Mr. Anderson
allows me to see my family. It is hard to be apart
from them. So, I make sure I am back on time."

"Did you blame James Johnson for your separation?"
Norvell continued. Jacob eyed them carefully. "Well I
recon you heard that I had some words with Johnson when
we were sold. He had said he would never divide a family
and yet that is what he did with us. So I was mad."

"Mad enough to kill him?" Key asked. "You must
have wanted some revenge for what he did."

"No sir, don't you go blaming his death on me." Jacob was
obviously agitated and kept looking to Anderson for help.

"We are not blaming you," said Norvell quickly. "Did
you notice anything unusual or out of place on your
way home as you were nearing Williamsburg?"

"No sir," Jacob quickly replied. "I keep my head down
and mind my own business. I didn't see nothing."

Norvell thanked Anderson for his time and asked
that he make Jacob available at the inquest Thursday
at 4 pm and for further discussions, if necessary.
Upon his return to the Wythe home, Key was told to

plan on a light supper about 7:30. "I have invited Thomas Jefferson to come over this evening so you two have a chance to meet," said Wythe. "Maybe he has some ideas. He is a terrific young man and very intuitive."

CHAPTER 10

After a short rest, Luck came downstairs to the family room a little before 7:30 PM. He was warmly greeted by Wythe who introduced him to Thomas Jefferson. Jefferson was studying law with Wythe, intending to become a lawyer and a political force in Virginia. Key noticed how tall Jefferson was as he stood next to him—at least 6 feet 4 inches. Like Mr. Wythe, Mr. Jefferson was dressed smartly but casually in a silk shirt and waistcoat. His long red hair was tied neatly behind him.

Wythe had told Key a little about Mr. Jefferson. He was twenty-two and owned considerable property of nearly 5,000 acres, including the family home at Shadwell, where his mother lived. His father Peter, of Welsh descent, had died when he was just fourteen and had left a large estate that was shared between Thomas and his younger brother Randolph. Thomas assumed full control for his share of the property when he turned twenty-one.

Thomas had received the type of education only available to the wealthiest plantation owners in Virginia. His father was self-taught and wanted more formal education for his sons, so Jefferson had tutors when he was a child and attended a small local English school with children from the surrounding plantations. He studied the classics, Latin, Greek and French and the natural world, which fascinated the inquisitive Jefferson.

At age sixteen Jefferson entered the College of William and

Mary in Williamsburg and began to collect a wide variety
of books to complement his formal education. He studied
mathematics, metaphysics and philosophy under the one
non-cleric on the faculty, Professor William Small, a friend
of Wythe. Mr. Jefferson loved music and was quite proficient,
learning to play the violin until he became skillful. Jefferson
enjoyed performing when provided an opportunity. He
graduated in two years and began his law studies under
Wythe's supervision. He also worked as his law clerk.

"You are a fortunate person Mr. Key to come under the
guidance of Master George Wythe," said Jefferson. "He has
been much more than a tutor for me as we have discussed
many aspects of life that go far beyond the practice of law. I
regard him as my second father, as I lost my own father when
I was fourteen. I understand you too lost your father at about
the same age. I am sorry for your loss, but know that you
will benefit greatly from the guidance of George Wythe."

The three men sat down to a light supper of cold roast pork,
cheese and ale. Supper was usually a casual affair with the
mid-afternoon dinner the bigger meal with all of the family
present. As they refreshed themselves, Wythe and Key provided
Jefferson with the details of the James Johnson murder.
Jefferson had heard rumors about the death, but no details, so
was very interested in both Wythe and Key's perspectives on
the crime. He seemed as puzzled as they were about the death.
Since Jefferson had agreed to serve with Wythe on the
inquest jury on Thursday, he said that he wanted to keep
an open mind about the cause and possible participants.
"However," said Jefferson, "it doesn't look like there will be
a satisfactory conclusion to the inquest, as it seems unlikely
that the Sheriff will be able to name a perpetrator."

"I know you are a friend of John Page," said Wythe. "He
also was close to James Johnson and they stayed at the
same guest house during the sessions of the House of
Burgesses. Apparently he has not been seen since Sunday.
Do you have any ideas of where he might be?"

"John and I were close during our days at the College of William and Mary," said Jefferson. "He and I spent most of late Sunday and Monday morning together. He actually stayed with me on Sunday night and then had to leave to deal with some personal issues. I know how he regarded James Johnson and he will be distraught when he gets the news."

Wythe nodded in agreement. "I have to think that Mr. Johnson's financial difficulty had something to do with his death. However his creditors would not wish him dead and I cannot understand who might benefit from his death."

They talked into the night, George and Tom regaling Luck with stories about their soirees with Governor Francis Fauquier at the Governor's Palace. Fauquier enjoyed hosting the Virginia elite at the Governor's Palace for dinner, which included the best of European wines and excellent foods—such as a baked lamb pastry, vegetables in sauces of cheese and herbs, and typical English deserts of pudding, followed by brandy. But he missed the repartee and intellectual debate that he was used to in England. Thus, he was in the habit of inviting Professor Small, George and recently Tom to the Governor's Palace for wide-ranging discussions on politics and the latest thinking from Europe on a variety of topics—philosophy, politics, and the arts. The liquor flowed freely and Jefferson said how much he enjoyed the discussions.

"They are entertaining and enlightening, yes," noted Wythe, "But sometimes I find myself wondering whether their main purpose is to try to elicit as much information about what the people are thinking in Virginia. Anyway, with increasing tensions between our elected leaders in the House of Burgesses and Parliament, I think it may be wise for us to be as discrete as possible."

"Well he did support the House of Burgesses on the Two Penny Act," said Jefferson, "and I think he is sympathetic to our position on the Stamp Act."

Luck asked Tom what the Two Penny Act was all about. "Well you know that tobacco is the main currency of payment in

Virginia. In 1757-58, due to unusually cold springs, followed
by two dry summers, the tobacco harvests were poor. The
House of Burgesses responded by passing the Two Penny Act.
The act provided that debts, contracts and salaries payable
in tobacco could instead be paid at the rate of exchange
of two pence per pound of leaf tobacco, because there was
not sufficient tobacco to honor the financial obligations
that required payment in tobacco. It was an emergency
measure and Governor Fauquier signed the legislation."

"I think most people felt that it was a reasonable response
to an emergency," continued Jefferson, "but the clergy were
hit hard by the act as they had been paid an annual stipend
of 16,000 pounds of tobacco, which was generally valued
higher than two pence per pound. The clergy argued that their
salaries had been cut by two-thirds—a bit of an exaggeration.
They sent their representatives to London and had the Two
Penny Act repealed by Parliament, to the consternation
of Governor Fauquier and the House of Burgesses."

"The Stamp Act situation is a little different," said Wythe.
"Last year it was rumored that to raise money to house
British troops in the colonies as a protection against Indian
uprisings, Parliament was going to pass a law requiring
official stamps on all documents, wills, contracts and
such. Well the colonies were incensed! In the past, there
was general agreement that Parliament could pass laws
with taxes pertaining to trade. Now they are claiming the
authority to impose purely domestic taxes on us."

"The colonies created 'Committees of Correspondence' to
draft a response to the possible action. I was chosen to draft the
letter for Virginia," said Wythe. "I think the Governor, when I
shared a draft with him, thought I had gone too far and urged
me to tone down the letter. Some of my Burgesses' colleagues
felt that as well, so we toned it down some. Still we produced
a strong statement of opposition arguing that we should
not be taxed on domestic matters without representation
in Parliament or approval by the House of Burgesses."

"What was Parliament's response?" asked Key.

"It was very discouraging," said Wythe. "There was no evidence that they even considered the position of the colonies or the letter from Virginia. I have heard that they claimed that since not everyone in England could vote for Parliament, we were in no worse position and that we had 'virtual' representation by all of the members. What nonsense! Virtual representation is effectively no representation. Unfortunately, this week the House of Burgesses was officially informed by the Governor that Parliament had passed the Stamp Act."

"It will certainly inflame the anti-Parliament sentiment," said Jefferson. "I think this was a terrible mistake by Parliament and will push Virginia closer to the more radical thinking of Boston and the New England colonies who are openly talking about breaking away from Great Britain. I must admit I am very dispirited about it but I don't think the Governor's opposition or support would have mattered much."

"Even though politics might be a bit strained with the Governor, he continues to entertain and hold musical events," said Jefferson. "I had a chance last winter to play as second violin in a quartet with the Governor. The Governor is quite accomplished on the harpsichord and we were joined by John Randolph, first violin, and Robert Carter, German flute. I am not that exceptional with the violin and it sometimes is a challenge for me, but I enjoy playing. I hope we don't give up our music occasions over politics!"

After being enjoined to demonstrate his playing ability, Tom reluctantly took out his violin and provided a delightful medley perfect for post-supper relaxation, before they all decided to call it an evening.

* * *

That same evening also found Sheriff Norvell discussing the case with Carter Braxton. The two men talked of the James Johnson murder and Norvell was particularly interested in Johnson's financial difficulties.

"I really am not aware that James Johnson's difficulties were any different than most of the other plantation owners," said Braxton. "We all struggle with debt and I think credit has tightened some with our current conflict over the Stamp Act. Perhaps London and Glasgow bankers are a bit more cautious about lending. They don't want to see open conflict that might affect the ability of plantation owners to repay their loans."

"In looking over Mr. Johnson's books, as provided by his Overseer Mechem, it seemed as if Johnson was in serious financial difficulty—perhaps more than the normal over-extension. Did he ever come to you for a loan or financial help?" asked Norvell.

"No. But he did ask me last year if I was interested in purchasing a few of his slaves, so that does suggest he was in a bind. I know he would not normally want to part with them. I told him that I was not able to buy more slaves at that time," said Braxton.

"Are you aware of the Negro Jacob that James Johnson sold to the Williamsburg blacksmith James Anderson." asked Norvell. "Apparently there was some trouble over the matter as Jacob's wife and children were sold to another planter."

"Jacob and his family were the Negroes James was asking me about," said Braxton. "He really wanted to sell the family as a unit, because he had made that promise to them. As I indicated to you, however, I told Johnson that I was not in a position to buy any more Negroes at the time. I might have been able to help him more had he come to me this year but I assumed he solved his problem last year."

"Are you aware of any other sources of credit that Mr. Johnson might have pursued?" followed up Norvell. Braxton thought and appeared to be a bit uncomfortable with the question. "It is possible that he might have tried to get a loan from Speaker John Robinson."

This surprised the Sheriff as plantation owners did not

usually loan funds to other owners, though it did happen occasionally. Robinson is an establishment fixture as the long-time Speaker of the House of Burgesses and also the Virginia Treasurer and he had his own significant personal resources. However, Norvell was astounded that Speaker Robinson would be loaning any significant money to other plantation owners, even if he was one of the wealthier planters. He owned more than 250 slaves and over 5,000 acres of land, but Norvell assumed that most of the Speaker's wealth was tied up in his property. Robinson had not said anything about making loans during their earlier discussion and Norvell thought he would have to have a more detailed conversation with Speaker Robinson about the loan issue.

As Norvell walked back to his lodgings just outside of Williamsburg, he thought through the revelation about Speaker Robinson. The Sheriff interacted with the Speaker quite often as he collected the local and colonial taxes and deposited the later with the Speaker as Robinson was also the Virginia Treasurer. Certainly Robinson had given him no indication that he lent out his funds to other plantation owners, nor had he heard that from others. He was not sure this had any bearing on the Johnson murder case, but he would follow through on this knowledge in future questions he might raise with other plantation owners.

CHAPTER 11

Thursday, May 23

On Wednesday Wythe had indicated to Key that he needed him for some work on Thursday, and Norvell was happy to allow him that latitude. Norvell said he had some things he wanted to follow-up on and would see Luck on Thursday afternoon at the Johnson Inquest.

Sheriff Norvell decided to meet with Speaker Robinson. He thought it was better for a conversation just between him and the Speaker. He guessed that there might be some sensitivity about the issue of lending funds to other plantation owners. He also had some private business that he had to attend to. He had collected taxes for the colony and needed to remit funds to the Treasurer, who was also the Speaker.

The loan issue might present some awkwardness in his relationship with the Speaker—not that he expected that the Speaker was a suspect in the case. The Speaker had just turned 60 and was suffering from a number of health issues. His frailty would have precluded an attack like the one sustained by Mr. Johnson. Still, Speaker Robinson had many friends in Virginia and there was always the possibility that there was some relationship between James Johnson's death and the funds Johnson hoped to procure while he was in Williamsburg. He found the Speaker in his small office in the Capitol Building. "More questions?" asked Robinson.

"A few," acknowledged Norvell, "but I also wanted to remit

to you and go over the first quarter receipts of the taxes."
Norvell had brought his journal, which contained a record of all
taxpayers in Williamsburg and James City County. While some
Sheriffs would simply mail in these reports, Norvell thought
it important to go over them with the Speaker, to provide
another set of eyes on the accounts and to allow Norvell to
explain any deficiencies in what was owed and what was paid.

"Lewis Burwell, a Member of the House of Burgesses from
James City County," said Norvell, "has asked for a three
month delay in payment of his owed taxes. As you know, his
plantation suffered a major fire late last year and it has taken
much of his capital to put things back together. I thought
this was appropriate. The Burwell holdings are significant
and I don't see any long-range problem with payment."

"I would agree with you," said Robinson.

Norvell then went over other lesser delinquencies,
which were mostly minor and created few problems.
"I do foresee a problem with the Stamp Act tax, if it is
enforced. I know this will not be the responsibility of
the Sheriff, but I expect that hatred of any tax is likely to
spill over to other taxes. I hope that won't happen."

Speaker Robinson agreed that it could be a potential
problem though he expressed his optimism that there
would be some compromise over the issue.

"I did have one other item I wanted to discuss with
you concerning the Johnson case," said Norvell.
"Carter Braxton mentioned that you sometimes
helped other plantation owners with loans."

Speaker Robinson grew angry. "Braxton should keep that kind
of information to himself." He quickly calmed down. "You are
probably aware that on Monday I led an effort in this session
to create a fund to provide emergency loans to plantation
owners, but that hothead Patrick Henry, who was barely
sworn in, made such a fuss about it in the House of Burgesses
that my proposal barely passed the House and was vetoed by
the Governor's Council. Henry claimed the proposal would

'reclaim the spendthrift from his dissipation and extravagance by filling his pockets with money.' What nonsense!"

"What Henry refused to recognize," said Robinson, "is that the plantation owners support the total economy in Virginia. Look up and down the streets of Williamsburg. Most of the shops are kept in business because of the patronage of plantation owners. So this proposal was really about the overall economy, not just some special benefit for a few planters."

Sheriff Norvell didn't comment. He tried to keep his own plantation afloat without too much debt, but knew he was only able to do so because of his income as Sheriff. Speaker Robinson reiterated that James Johnson had not approached him for a loan. Norvell thanked the Speaker and told him that he would keep him informed about progress on the case.

While in the Capitol Building Norvell happened upon Robert Carter III, an attorney and member of the Governor's Council. He decided that he might inquire about his knowledge of Mr. Johnson and the Speaker's lending practices. While the two of them were not of the same social standing, they had known each other for many years and were on a first name basis.

Norvell also knew that Carter was one of the few plantation owners who had been actively speaking about ending slavery in Virginia. He talked about it openly and viewed slavery as a moral evil. While he tried to advocate for its elimination in the Governor's Council, he did not find a responsive ear to his views. He had freed some of his slaves, providing them places to live and acres to farm from his own plantation land and was talking about trying to find a way to free all of the slaves that worked at his plantation.

"What brings you to the Capitol Building, William," Carter asked. "It is always good to see you, but I suspect you have some business to discuss."

"It is good to see you too. How is your large family doing? My daughter is still in England and I miss having her here with me in Williamsburg," said Norvell.

"William, to answer your question, everyone is fine, but

I think it is time you considered getting married again. You have an excellent position and could attract a good match if you wanted to," Carter responded. "I usually don't play matchmaker, but in your case I would be glad to keep my eyes open for an appropriate match. It is not healthy or wise for you to be alone so much of the time."

"That is kind of you to say Robert," replied Norvell. "I have not given any serious consideration to marrying again. I suspect that when my daughter Johanna returns from England she will want to be the mistress of the house."

"My main reason for seeking you out is that I wanted to ask your advice about the James Johnson murder case that I am working on. I know you knew Johnson somewhat, but you may not have known that he was deeply in debt—more than the usual over extension that we face occasionally. I can't figure out how that would figure in the murder and yet there doesn't seem any other significant motive. I also have discovered that Speaker Robinson sometimes lent funds to other plantation owners, but again, how does that fact fit with the murder?"

Carter took some time to think over the question before answering. "One of the evils of slavery," he said, "is that plantation owners spend beyond their means to buy more slaves in hopes of larger crops. So not only do we demean the Negroes making the slaves our property but we demean ourselves by acting wealthier than we really are and as a result many of the plantation owners take on more debt than they should. I can see that creating problems, though how that ties in specifically with the Johnson murder I can't provide an answer. Would you like me to discretely ask other members of the Governor's Council about this?"

"Thank you Robert," said Norvell. "I would appreciate any information that you find out that might affect the case. Obviously this is sensitive. The murder did not involve a bar-room brawl, or a jealous husband, or any of the usual motives that I can determine. The case is still new but we have yet to come up with a plausible motive for the death. We are having the inquest this afternoon."

The two men wished each other well and promised to get together soon for dinner. Carter indicated that he would get back to Norvell if he found any information that might be useful.

CHAPTER 12

The Inquest

The official James Johnson Inquest was held at the Williamsburg Courthouse at 4 pm Thursday afternoon, presided over by Dr. John Minson Galt in his role as city and county coroner. The Inquest Jury consisted of George Wythe, Thomas Jefferson, House of Burgesses members Carter Braxton from King William County and Edward Champion Travis, from Jamestown. The fifth member was Anthony Hay, the owner of the Raleigh Tavern.

The Courthouse was designed in a "Georgian Style" common to official buildings of the period and prominently located on the Duke of Gloucester Street, between the Palace Green and Queen Street. It was built of red bricks with white wooden trim-boards and long arched windows with white shutters. A projected portico over the entrance provided some cover from the elements. Inside was a place for the judge, in this case the coroner, Dr. Galt, a jury box, and seating for witnesses and guests who were interested in the case. In the audience were those witnesses expected to be called to testify at the inquest, including Sheriff Norvell, Luck Key and John Mechem. Mrs. Johnson did not attend; however, her daughter Bethany was present. Luck admired Bethany's beauty. She was wearing black and in mourning for her father, yet her composure and refinement were remarkable. Some other

members of the House of Burgesses were in the audience as well
as some of the town merchants who knew Mr. Johnson. James
Anderson also showed up and brought Jacob with him, as the
Sheriff had requested. John Page had received a message about
the death of his friend and also had come back for the inquest.

"In many cases the jury would examine the body," said Dr.
Galt. "However in this case I felt that this was not necessary,
as I can describe the injury in sufficient detail for the jury."
After explaining his findings as a doctor and coroner on the
nature of the wound and probable time of death, he called
George Wythe as first witness to provide testimony.

Wythe explained that on Monday morning he had awoke
to the news that a man had been killed in the Powder
Magazine. He explained how his new junior clerk Luck
Key had found the body and come for him. In turn, he had
sent for Dr. Galt and they had met at the Powder Magazine
to discover the body of James Johnson a member of the
House of Burgesses from King William County.

"What did you notice about the death?" asked Galt.

"Mr. Johnson appeared to have been struck from behind," said
Wythe. "There was a large gash on his back running from the
right shoulder blade diagonally towards the left side. There
was considerable blood loss and the blood had dried. The limbs
were stiffening, suggesting that Mr. Johnson had been dead for
some time, at least a few hours. You and I also noticed that it
looked like Mr. Johnson's clothes had been looked through,
perhaps for something tying Johnson to the murderer."

"I asked you to secure the scene before you took the body
away and I instructed my junior clerk Mr. Key to ride to
Jamestown and inform the Sheriff so that he might take charge
of the investigation. Mr. Key came back to my house and I
provided him a horse to ride to Jamestown," concluded Wythe.

Galt next called Luck Key to the stand. This was the
third time Key had been in a court. The first dealt with his
apprenticeship and the second when he came of age and the
estate was settled. Still he was a bit nervous and did not

want to look bad in front of Mr. Wythe or Bethany Johnson.
He retold his story, which Wythe had already explained.

"Did you know the victim?" asked Galt.

"No sir," said Key. "This was my first time in Williamsburg
and I am quite sure that I had never met Mr. Johnson in
the past. I grew up and lived in Louisa County. I did meet
Patrick Henry once and I had met Mr. Wythe, but I do not
know any other members of the House of Burgesses."

Galt questioned why Key had gone into the Powder Magazine.
"As I told Mr. Wythe and the Sheriff, I was curious. At first, I just
wanted to get a closer look at the Powder Magazine, but then I
noticed that the door was open so anyone could enter and that
did not seem right. I guess I thought I would find out about it
and then tell Mr. Wythe." said Key. "Of course I never expected
to find a body. It was quite a shock, and after determining
that the person was indeed dead, I went as quickly as possible
to Mr. Wythe's house to inform him of the situation."

Key stepped down, relieved that his role was finished and
he could relax a bit and take in the rest of the testimony. Galt
next called Sheriff William Norvell. The Sheriff related that Mr.
Key had found him in Jamestown and they had hurried back to
Williamsburg where Norvell took charge of the investigation.

"Dr. Galt, you had the body removed before I arrived and you
secured the scene." said Norvell. "I asked Mr. Wythe and Mr. Key
to help me search the Powder Magazine and we found the likely
murder weapon, a halberd with a sharp hatchet-like blade
just below the point; it had blood on the blade. We found boot
prints but they were not recognizable, although probably a
man's boot. I did also find some tobacco juice stains by the door,
but again it did not provide any real knowledge of the culprit.
There was a small pistol found on the floor, which was probably
Mr. Johnson's. That might suggest that he was somewhat
cautious about the meeting—perhaps he sensed some danger."

Sheriff Norvell explained that he next examined the body,
which Dr. Galt had moved to a shed behind the apothecary.
"The wound was consistent with the halberd that we

found. This is an unusual weapon and suggests that the perpetrator might not have been adept at using swords or other possible weapons. However, it is possible that it was just something easy to reach as a weapon, perhaps not planned beforehand but grabbed on the spur of the moment."

"Did you come to any conclusions about the perpetrator?" asked Galt.

"A halberd is a heavy weapon, and the blow was struck at an angle, likely from a tall person, swinging the halberd from the right side, down against the back of Mr. Johnson. I expect the death was nearly immediate, given the depth of the wound. It seems unlikely that a woman could have wielded that weapon in such a manner, so I would think the person who murdered James Johnson was a man and probably right handed, given the nature of the blow," continued the Sheriff.

"Mr. Key and I rode out to Johnson's Plantation in the afternoon to inform Mrs. Johnson," stated Norvell. "We interviewed both Mrs. Johnson and the plantation overseer, John Mechem, the next day. No one could understand who might have committed this murder. Johnson apparently carried nothing of substantial value that would have prompted the murder. Mr. Mechem did make me aware of a quarrel that occurred a few months ago when Mr. Johnson sold five of his slaves. Unfortunately, he had to separate a family and the male head of the family, Jacob, said some threatening words."

"Mr. Key and I interviewed Jacob yesterday and I have asked him to be here for this inquest," continued Norvell. "He admits to having words with Mr. Johnson, but claims that he had nothing to do with his death. He is now owned by the blacksmith, James Anderson. Jacob has no alibi for the likely time of Mr. Johnson's death. Mr. Anderson had lent him a horse to see his family, which he apparently did every other Sunday. No one knows exactly when he returned to his lodgings. Mr. Anderson also has promised Jacob his freedom after seven years working with the blacksmith."

"The other matter that the jury should be aware of is

that Mr. Mechem said he thought that Mr. Johnson was
meeting someone this weekend to borrow some funds or
to otherwise help financially. Creditors had been pressing
Johnson, which was the reason he had to sell the slaves last
year. And it does seem probably that he went to the Powder
Magazine to meet someone late Sunday night or early
Monday morning. So at this point," concluded Norvell, "I
believe this is a clear case of murder, probably by a man, but
otherwise can offer no judgment as to the perpetrator."

Galt next called John Mechem, Johnson's Overseer. He
confirmed that the plantation was in some financial difficulty
but Mr. Johnson had told him that he had a possible solution.
Unfortunately, Mechem could provide no more details on
who Mr. Johnson intended to meet with. When asked about
the altercation during the sale of the slaves, Mechem said:
"Jacob and his family were quite upset about being separated
and they had words. I would not have put up with it, but Mr.
Johnson was always a bit soft when it came to treatment
of his slaves and left most of that responsibility to me."

"Do you remember what specifically was said," asked Galt.

"I don't really remember all of the details, but I remember
Jacob saying something like 'you will live to regret
this'. It was an obvious threat. I guess we never thought
Jacob would take this kind of action," said Mechem.

There were audible murmurs in the courthouse as many
turned to look at Jacob, who looked shocked. "I never said
that!" yelled Jacob as he was restrained by Anderson.

Galt dismissed Mechem and called Jacob to
the stand. "I do not want any lies from you," said
Galt. "What did you tell Mr. Johnson?"

"I told him that he had promised to not separate families
if he had to sell any of us," said Jacob, who was visibly
shaking. "I was mad and told him he was going back against
his word and pleaded with him to sell me with my family.
He told me he was sorry, that he tried to sell us as a family,
but could not do that and had to sell me separately."

"Did you threaten to kill Mr. Johnson," asked Galt. Some in the crowd yelled out "Murderer!"

"No sir, I did not!" exclaimed Jacob. "Why would I do such a thing? I would never be able to see my family again." As Jacob stepped back to his place next to Anderson, there were calls for the Sheriff to arrest him.

"Calm down, everyone," Sheriff Norvell quickly asserted his presence. He was not likely to be challenged. "No one is going to be arrested until we have a finding from the Inquest Jury."

Bethany Johnson stood up and addressed Dr. Galt. "Sir, I have some information for this inquest. My name is Bethany Johnson and I am the only child of my father James Johnson."

Dr. Galt had not met her before and immediately said how sorry everyone was for her loss. "What can you tell us about this horrible event?"

"Jacob's wife Sally was my maid and was like an older sister to me when I was young. So I too was distraught at my father having to sell Jacob and his family. I pleaded with him not to sell the family, but he told me that he had no choice because of the family finances. I was present when they were led away and can say for certain that Jacob never threatened my father."

"Were you there the entire time," asked Galt.

"I think so sir," said Miss Johnson. "I just don't believe that Jacob would kill my father. He is a proud man but never has shown any violence to anyone."

"Thank you Miss Johnson for your testimony," said Dr. Galt. "I appreciate how difficult this must be for you." "Is there anyone else that has testimony to provide regarding the death of James Johnson?" asked Galt. Hearing none, Dr. Galt turned to the jury and asked them to convene and determine their findings.

The Inquest Jury convened in a small side-room off the main courthouse room. Carter Braxton was the first to speak. "Well it looks to me like Jacob had the only motive and opportunity to do this crime. He also was more likely to grab a halberd than use another weapon and he is tall and strong enough to inflict the type of wound described. I am inclined to name him as the probable murderer."

"That seems unlikely to me," said Wythe. "Why would Johnson agree to meet Jacob at the Powder Magazine at midnight? By himself? I can't understand why he would have done that."

"I wish we knew who James Johnson was planning to meet with about his debts," said Jefferson. "Perhaps they could shed some more light on the events. Though if someone planned to lend him money, why would he strike Johnson down? That also makes no sense. However the fact that no one has come forward regarding the debt is also to me a bit suspicious. As to the weapon, it may suggest someone unskilled in the use of the other arms, but also could have been used to confuse the investigation."

"I am afraid we will not be able to return a specific finding in terms of who murdered Johnson," said Anthony Hay, the owner of the Raleigh Tavern. "This would have been much simpler if there had been a drunken fight in my tavern with many witnesses. Here, with no witnesses or clear motive, there are only possibilities." The others nodded their agreement.

"It looks like our findings will be 'death by murder by an unknown perpetrator'," said Wythe. "Are we all agreed on that?" They all nodded yes, though Carter Braxton did so reluctantly. They went back into the courtroom and provided their findings to Dr. Galt, who made them official and announced that the Johnson Inquest was concluded and urged the Sheriff to attempt to find the perpetrator and bring him to justice. Norvell agreed, but worried that they might never know for sure who was guilty of the crime, given the lack of evidence as to whom Mr. Johnson was meeting with or even a likely motive.

Luck saw Bethany outside the Courthouse and walking over to her gently told her he thought she was very brave to confront Mechem in court. "I get so mad at Mr. Mechem, sometimes," said Miss Johnson. "I know that my father had to restrain or admonish him sometimes on his treatment of our slaves. I have seen him beating them though he tried to hide that from my father. Father was a gentle man and always tried to do what was best for them. Jacob and Sally were almost like family and we all were sad when my father had to sell them. I so detest slavery. I understand we could not have our plantation without them. Still it does not seem to be right. In fact how can we morally hold another person as our slave?"

"You sound like an abolitionist," said Key.

"So what if I am?" asked Miss Johnson. "I just hope that at some point all the slaves will be free. That is what I wish for. You probably think I am just a foolish girl," she said.

"Not at all," replied Luck. "You are to be commended for your strong feelings. I have to admit that I am somewhat conflicted by the issue. I have never owned a slave and my parents did not either. I have never really considered the morality of slavery. But how do you operate a large plantation without slaves?"

"You men will have to figure it out," said Bethany. "I hope you and Sheriff Norvell can find the person who killed my father."

"We certainly will try our best," said Luck bravely reassuring her, though he was not at all confident that they could accomplish the task.

Luck saw Sheriff Norvell, who motioned him over. Bethany also came over and on behalf of her mother extended an invitation to dinner on Sunday for both Key and Norvell. On a more serious matter, Bethany also asked the Sheriff if they needed to keep her father's remains or whether they could be released to the family. Norvell said that he would speak with Dr. Galt, but with the inquest now closed he assumed that the remains would be released to the family. "Would you like me to handle that for you?"

"Thank you so much," said Bethany. "My father was not particularly religious and, given the nature of his death, we plan to hold a private ceremony at the plantation and bury him there."

Norvell indicated that he thought he could have her father's remains taken to the plantation tomorrow. He and

Luck readily accepted the invitation to the plantation on
Sunday for dinner and Bethany left to find her carriage for
the long ride back to Rosebud. She would have to stop at
a friend's plantation on the way back to spend the night as
it would have been impossible to return before dark.

"She is an amazing young woman," said Norvell, "But we have
to consider the possibility that her affection for her maid Sally
clouded her views about what Jacob actually said. Revenge is a
possible motive. Still, I can't imagine James Johnson agreeing to
meet with Jacob at midnight, unless Jacob got him there under
some ruse. Even if Jacob did not kill Johnson, I feel that he has
not been fully truthful with us. I would like you to talk with
him; he might have seen something helpful to the investigation.
Perhaps a one-on-one conversation would be less intimidating
than both of us confronting him. He might confide in you."

They agreed to meet in the morning and see what their
next steps would be. Norvell suggested that they both
try to think about other possible people who might have
a bearing on the case. Before heading to his lodgings,
Norvell saw Dr. Galt, complemented him on the conduct
of the inquest and asked about releasing Johnson's body
to the family. Galt said that should be no problem.

"May I ask you a favor?" said Norvell. "I would appreciate
it if you could make the necessary arrangements. A fairly
nice coffin would be appropriate and please see if you can
arrange for someone to take the remains out to the Johnson
plantation. Don't worry about the expense, I will take care
of it. It seems the least we can do for the family given the
untimely death and their apparent financial situation."

"That is a very kind gesture," said Galt. "Yes, I would
be glad to take care of it for you as I know you are
tied up in the investigation. I hope you can find the
guilty party and bring closure to this affair."

✳ ✳ ✳

As George Wythe was leaving he caught up with John Page to see if he could shed any light on the mystery. He doubted that, as Page did not volunteer any information at the inquest. Still he thought it appropriate to make sure they knew whatever Page did. "John, I was at Mrs. George's guest house earlier this week and tried to catch you, but Mrs. George indicated that you had left Sunday, she thought for your plantation."

"Yes, I did have some business that I had to deal with," said Page, "but I was so sorry to hear about James Johnson. I was probably closer to him than anyone else in the House of Burgesses."

"So you left Sunday for your plantation?" asked Wythe.

"No, actually I had planned a late night with Tom Jefferson and ended up staying in his housing room Sunday night and leaving on Monday. So I don't really have any information on why James went to the Powder Magazine on Sunday night. I only wish I had known about it and gone with him. Perhaps I could have prevented the tragedy."

"You probably knew that Mr. Johnson was concerned about finances and it is possible the meeting was about that topic. Did he confide in you as to whom he might have approached to borrow funds or otherwise assist in solving his financial crises?" asked Wythe.

"He did question me some regarding the rumors that Speaker Robinson had assisted some plantation owners with loans, but I told him that I really did not know the details regarding that practice," responded Page.

George Wythe thanked Mr. Page and left wondering if Page had revealed the whole story. John Page was himself a wealthy plantation owner, the great-great-grandson of Col. John Page, an early founder of Virginia and one of its richest men in the 1600s. Their plantation Rosewood, in Gloucester County, was on the York River. Col. Page had provided the bulk of the funding for the Burton Parish Church and also had been involved in selecting the site and in funding the College of William and

Mary. John Page was born in Rosewood, the son of Alice and Mann Page, who had inherited much of the family fortune. If James Johnson was in financial trouble, why wouldn't he ask his friend John Page for assistance? It may be that the son had little independent funds apart from his likely inheritance from his father. Wythe thought he would have to provide this information to Sheriff Norvell to see what he could make of it.

CHAPTER 13

Friday, May 24

After the dismal day on Thursday, Friday was bright with flowers and trees blooming and the sounds of spring in the air. It seemed like all of Williamsburg was aflame in color. Sheriff Norvell met Luck at Wythe's house and before they left, George Wythe told him the information that he had received from John Page. "I think he may know more than he is saying," stated Wythe, "but I'll let you take charge of that."

Luck and the Sheriff began to walk across the Palace Green and discussed how to proceed. "As I mentioned yesterday," said Norvell, "I would like you to again visit with Jacob, It does seem like he was returning about the same time the murder occurred. Perhaps he saw something and may not have realized its significance. We can't rule out Jacob for the murder, but I don't see how he would have persuaded Mr. Johnson to come at night to the Powder Magazine. Also, ask around among the merchants to see if they saw or heard anything unusual. Again, they may be reluctant to say anything, but I can't help but feel that someone has information that might be useful for us."

"I will spend some more time talking to members of the House of Burgesses. They might respond privately to me, especially if they feel there are political issues involved. Let's reconvene at dinner about 3 pm and we can compare notes as to what we have found," Norvell concluded. "Mr. Wythe has kindly invited us to dine with him and perhaps together we can make some sense of this matter."

* * *

Luck's first stop was to the Shoemaker Shop, located on the same square as the Powder Magazine. George Wilson, who had recently moved to Williamsburg from Norfolk, was the proprietor. This was a typical Williamsburg shop, with the store on the ground level and a living area on the second floor. Wilson specialized in "Boots and Shoes for Gentlemen," and he carried a variety of shoes, both "off the shelf" and custom made. This was a prestigious business which catered to the elite in Virginia society. Key was welcomed by the proprietor and he explained his responsibility for investigating the death of James Johnson.

"It is so sad," said Wilson, "I knew Mr. Johnson for a couple of years and provided shoes both for him and his Overseer John Mechem. They are both fine gentlemen."

"Since your shop is so close to the Powder Magazine," said Key, "I am hoping that you might have heard or noticed something that would be helpful in our investigation."

"I have thought about this ever since I heard about the murder," said Wilson. "But I can't really think of anything that seemed strange or out of place. Of course, since the House of Burgesses is in session, you had your usual noise level from drinking and general conversation. But I don't recall any loud arguments or other noise."

Key thanked Mr. Wilson for his help and spent a bit of time admiring some of his handiwork. "I could offer you a good deal on some of these shoes in stock," said Wilson. "I also noticed that you have a slight limp. It might be that a specialized set of boots would help correct the problem."

"That is very kind of you," said Key, "however, I must decline for now as my income and resources are too meager to afford a nice pair of shoes or boots, let alone ones that are specially fitted. Still, perhaps in the future I can call on you again."

Walking across the Duke of Gloucester Street, he went into Chowning's Tavern, almost directly across the street from the Powder Magazine. Owner Josiah Chowning had place a sign next to the front door, the nature of which was included in a recent advertisement in the Virginia *Gazette*:

> *I HEREBY acquaint the publick that I have opened a tavern at the house where I formerly lived, where all who please to favour me with their custom may depend upon the best of entertainment for themselves, servants, and horses, and good pasturage.*

As a new "ale house," Chowning's was not as big as some of the other established taverns but Mr. Wythe had told Luck that it enjoyed a good reputation for hearty and reasonably priced food and drink. He found Josiah Chowning behind the bar and explained that he was working for the Sheriff on the murder of James Johnson. Luck noted that Mr. Chowning seemed a perfect ale house owner, a bit short and stout with an infectious grin that would warm potential customers. However at the mention of the murder, Mr. Chowning grew quiet, his grin replaced with a frown.

"Sunday nights are not as busy as Fridays or Saturdays," noted Chowning. "We had about a dozen people in for dinner and drinks, but we wound down by about eleven. From then until midnight, I was cleaning up."

"Do you remember who was here on Sunday night?" asked Key.

"We had a couple of members of the House of Burgesses and their friends. I remember Burgesses Edmund Chiswell, John Page and Richard Adams being here. I didn't recognize everyone but I assumed most were here for business with the legislature or Governor," said Chowning.

"Did you hear or see anything coming from the square about

midnight?" asked Key.

"No, I didn't," said Chowning. "I am sorry I can't help you. I didn't know Mr. Johnson well, but it is shocking that a murder could happen right here in Williamsburg, just across the street."

Luck thanked Mr. Chowning and said they might have to return for additional information but he appreciated all that he could relate about that Sunday evening. Luck also asked at a couple of the other neighboring shops but no one could shed any light on their problem.

*　*　*

About one in the afternoon, Key went by the Blacksmith's shop. He timed it so that Jacob would probably be due a break for dinner and he wanted to catch him in a more relaxed situation. As expected, Jacob was just beginning to take an hour break. Bypassing the blacksmith, Luck drew up to Jacob and asked if he could talk to him.

"I want to ensure you that neither Sheriff Norvell nor I think you are guilty of this murder," said Key. "We are hopeful that you might have some information that would be useful to us."

Jacob reluctantly agreed. He suggested they sit out in the garden behind the Blacksmith Shop where there was a bench that was his typical spot for taking a break. James Anderson and the white apprentices would all be heading to their homes for dinner, so there would be no one to bother or overhear them.

"It is quite lovely here," said Key. "I can see why you like this spot." They were surrounded by trees and gardens, now almost in full bloom. When Jacob only nodded, Key went on, "tell me about your work and your family's work at the Johnson plantation?"

"I know some people think I must have murdered Mr. Johnson, but that is not true. He was a good master. He bought me at a slave auction in Norfolk when I was just a boy, kidnapped and sold off a slave ship from Africa. I hardly knew any English but what I learned on the boat. I noticed then that Mr. Johnson was different from other slave owners. He had a carriage and I was allowed to ride in the back on the way to the plantation. He didn't shackle me and told me that if I worked hard he would take good care of me. As I grew, he taught me English and gave me more responsibilities—that's how I learned blacksmithing. I married one of the house maids Sally and he helped build a separate house for us and for our family when we had children. So he was a good man, but he had promised never to separate us and he did that," said Jacob.

"You must have blamed Mr. Johnson for the sale," hinted Luck.

"If I had to blame anyone it would be John Mechem. He became the overseer just a few years ago and things were not the same after that. He often beat the slaves, especially when Mr. Johnson was away. He kept away from me generally as I think he knew that Mr. Johnson respected me. It was Mechem who suggested that Mr. Johnson needed to sell some of the slaves because of the plantation's financial situation. And he specifically suggested our family because he thought we would generate the most funds, but I really think he wanted to get rid of me so he could do what he wanted with the other slaves."

Luck thought this was very interesting information, though it was unclear how it might relate to the murder. "Could you just take me through your day last Sunday, when you left Williamsburg, how long were you gone, what you did, and exactly when you got home?" asked Key."

Jacob began his story: "I got up early, as I usually do when I go to see my Sally and our three children—about six, I guess. Mr. Anderson provides me a note that I have his permission to go to William Moore's plantation near Yorktown. It takes me 'bout three hours or so to get there by horse. Usually if I go early on Sunday, I don't meet no one and that was true last Sunday. I try to get there in time for Sunday services, which are about ten or so. Isiah, one of Moore's slaves, is able to read the Bible and he reads some from the holy book and we sing and afterwards I have time to be with my family. They always try to prepare something nice for me and I try to bring something for them. Mrs. Anderson sometimes gives me a special treat to take them, like a minced or apple pie. Mr. and Mrs. Anderson are very good to me."

"Well the afternoon is a time all my children tell me about what they are doing and how they are getting on," continued Jacob. "My oldest is trying to learn how to read from Isiah. Isiah says he won't live forever and needs to have some young eyes reading the Bible. The two youngest mainly play with the small children of Mr. Moore as they are not big enough to do much work in the tobacco fields. My wife Sally is a maid to the oldest Moore daughter. Round 'bout eight we have a little supper and then I have to begin the trip back to Williamsburg. This is always the hardest part, both for me and for them. We can't help but cry about the separation. I know Mr. Johnson said he had no choice and had to sell us separately, but it still is a very bitter memory. I liked Master Johnson, however he shouldn't have done that."

"I know that makes me look bad, that maybe I was so mad I would strike at Mr. Johnson," continued Jacob. "But by the love of Jesus, I did not and would not. I really blame Mechem more than Mr. Johnson. Now with Mr. Anderson I have some hope for a future where I might be free and might be able to purchase the freedom of my family. If I were hanged none of that would happen." Jacob was quiet for a moment, flooded with emotions about his family and for a possible future where he might be free. "I would do nothing to risk losing that possibility," he said.

Luck thought to himself that he believed Jacob's story. "What time did you get back to Williamsburg and from which direction did you arrive?" asked Key.

"I think I got back about half before midnight," said Jacob. "The road from Yorktown comes through the south of town, so I rode up South England Street and then made my way to the stables located behind the Blacksmith's Shop near Francis Street. Everything was fairly quiet, it was late and while there was the usual noise from the taverns along Duke of Gloucester

Street, I didn't see anyone. After taking care of the horse, I went to the shed behind the Blacksmith's Shop where I have my bed and things."

Luck was quiet for a bit, thinking about Jacob's comments. Obviously his timing could be checked with the people at the Moore Plantation, but even if everything Jacob said was true, he still could have met James Johnson at the Powder Magazine around midnight. "When you were riding up South England Street you were almost directly in line with the Powder Magazine," said Key. "So I would ask you to think carefully and tell me if you saw anything that seemed out of place, or unusual."

Jacob thought and became a bit agitated. "No one is going to believe a slave anyway," said Jacob, "so why should I talk any more. I have told you what you wanted to know. Anything more will just get me into trouble."

"Jacob, some people think you killed Mr. Johnson," said Key. "I don't believe that you did, but we need to find who really did murder the man so that you will not have this shadow over you."

"I guess when you put the issue that way, and I don't know whether it means anything, but I did see a horse hitched to the back fence near Francis Street. I guess it just surprised me, as it was not in front of a tavern or house." said Jacob.

"What kind of horse?" asked Key, "Can you describe it?"

"I think it was a dark Roan," said Jacob, "but am not sure I could describe it any better, or recognize it for sure. There was some starlight, but I didn't really look at it for very long. I don't know whether this is helpful or not. I have only seen a few Roan horses, but it looked like that type of horse."

Luck thanked Jacob and said that he appreciated his candor. He knew that there were likely many horses in the area of the same general type, still it did give them some information on whom James Johnson was likely meeting. A Roan is rarer than a typical Virginia horse and is a characterized by an even mixture of colored and white hairs on the body, while the head, lower legs, mane and tail are mostly solid color, gray, black or white.

Since Jacob described it as dark, he suspected the dominant solid color was gray, dark brown or black.

CHAPTER 14

While Luck was interviewing merchants and talking to Jacob, Sheriff Norvell went to the Capitol Building to try to speak with some of the members of the House of Burgesses. There was talk that the session was winding down and he wanted to make sure that he talked to as many members as possible to try to understand the possible reasoning behind the late night meeting that led to James Johnson's murder. He first sought out Henry Lee, someone Norvell held in high regard.

Richard Henry Lee was regarded by some as the "Cicero" of the House of Burgesses. Born in Westmoreland County and educated in England, Lee returned to Virginia in 1751 following the death of his parents. His father Thomas Lee was the governor of Virginia before his death and the family came from a line of military officers, diplomats and legislators. Henry Lee was appointed Justice of Peace from Westmoreland County in 1757 and elected to the House of Burgesses a year later. Like Richard Carter, Lee was opposed to slavery and condemned the institution as contrary to Christian values. His first speech was in support of slowing the importation of slaves to Virginia and he quickly gained a reputation as one of the most eloquent and passionate members of the House.

Norvell remembered that during the Stamp Act dispute, Lee initially thought to apply for one of the Stamp distributor jobs, but his fellow Virginian George Mercer, who was in London at the time, was awarded the post. While some would complain that it was only sour grapes, Lee eventually became a strong opponent of the Act. Norvell felt that his change of heart was legitimate as Lee became convinced that the Act would have long term negative consequences on the operations of Virginia and the ability of the people to govern themselves on domestic matters.

In November 1764 Mr. Lee convinced the House of Burgesses to protest the Act with a message to the King and was involved with George Wythe in the Committee on Correspondence, which drafted the message, insisting that the British constitution guaranteed that British subjects could not be taxed without their consent.

Sheriff Norvell was interested in whether the murdered man had also been involved in the Stamp Act controversy and whether that might have played a role in his death. Taking him aside in the Capitol Building, Norvell probed for any possible connection.

"James Johnson was generally a passive observer during most of the controversy," said Lee. "His sympathies were with the conservative planters and most of them did not want to jeopardize Virginia's relationship with Parliament. I had the feeling he was not 'unsympathetic' with our cause, but he did not want to stick his neck out unnecessarily. Johnson generally sided with his Prince William colleague, Carter Braxton, and he was not involved in drafting the resolutions in opposition that came from the Committee on Correspondence. But he never spoke out against us. I felt that he did not want to be involved in the debate, perhaps antagonizing his more conservative colleagues in the House."

"Mr. Johnson was deeply in debt," continued Norvell. "He had to sell some slaves last year and may have had to sell land this year. He seemed to feel that he had some financial prospects to shore up his finances, but I don't know what they were or whether they could be related to his death. Would you have any idea?" asked Norvell.

Lee considered the question. "Can you keep some information I am going to give you confidential?" asked Lee.

"I can certainly try," said Norvell. "You understand that if it has bearing on the death in question, I or you might have to provide testimony in court about the matter."

"Yes, certainly," said Lee. "Well you may know that some planters have received loans from Speaker Robinson. And there has been some concern that all of the funds used for the loans were not coming from Robinson's personal account. I have heard a rumor that some Glasgow merchants trading in Virginia complained to the Lords of Trade in England about un-burned notes in the colony's treasury. You may remember that notes were issued by England to pay certain debts of the plantation owners in return for tobacco. As they were redeemed by the Treasury, they were supposed to be destroyed, and not remain in circulation, which would have the effect allowing the notes to be used twice. Anyway, that was the intent."

"In 1763 House of Burgesses members Richard Bland, Benjamin Harrison and I prepared a report to the House finding the accounts all in order," said Lee. "But the rumors persist and in December of last year our three members were asked to look into it further with a bigger committee formed. Our investigation has been delayed, however we expect to do a more detailed accounting after the session of the House of Burgesses. You know I am not a supporter of the Speaker. He has for too long favored the large planters at the expense of others. And he has continued to follow the more conservative legislators on matters pertaining to England. Still, how this ties to the Johnson death, I could not begin to guess." concluded Lee.

"Is there someone close to the Speaker that I should try to talk to?" asked Norvell, "I have already spoken to Speaker Robinson about this matter and he seemed rather hesitant to share information he possessed. But he claimed that Mr. Johnson had never approached him for a loan."

"You might want to talk to Edmund Chiswell of Middlesex County," said Lee. "He is Speaker Robinson's brother-in-law and

since Robinson's marriage to Susanna Chiswell, Edmund has
some influence, perhaps undue influence, over the Speaker on
financial matters. He follows the Speaker's views politically."

Norvell thanked Lee and headed off to find Chiswell. Edmund
Chiswell's family was originally from Hanover County and he
had fared well since his sister married John Robinson. His background was common among the Virginia planters. His family
had arrived from England in the mid-1600s and gradually built
their fortunes on tobacco, in Chiswell's case in Hanover and
then Middlesex County.

Norvell considered Edmund Chiswell to be among the Virginia elites, more by lineage than wealth. Although since his sister married Robinson, Chiswell had seen his prospects brighten,
as Speaker Robinson had helped him to enlarge his plantation in
Middlesex County.

When Norvell found Mr. Chiswell he was speaking to his
brother-in-law, Speaker Robinson. "Well, here comes the Sheriff
again," said Speaker Robinson. "You haven't come to arrest us
for anything have you?" Robinson joked.

"Do you need arresting for something?" Norvell shot back
with a laugh. "No actually, I wanted to talk to Mr. Chiswell for a
few minutes if you can spare him."

"Of course," answered Robinson. "Edmund, I will see you at
dinner." He took his leave of Chiswell and Norvell.
Sheriff Norvell briefly explained that he was investigating
James Johnson's murder and hoped Chiswell might shed some
light on the situation.

"I don't see how I can help you," said Chiswell.

"Even so," said Norvell, "I would like you to tell me about your
relationship with Mr. Johnson and whether you know of any
reason that someone might want to harm him."

"I can't say that we really had a close relationship," said Chiswell somewhat arrogantly. "Of course I knew him as a fellow
Burgesses, however, he was not really in our social orbit. I may
have dined with him a few times over the course of the legislative sessions, but we were always discussing the political issues

of the day. I thought he was a bit provincial, perhaps not up to his leadership position."

"What were Mr. Johnson's political views? Was he aligned with you and the Speaker or more with Henry Lee and Patrick Henry?" asked Norvell.

"That is a good question," Chiswell answered. "Mr. Johnson kept his own counsel, although he was influenced by Carter Braxton, his colleague from King William County, and also by his friend John Page, so in that sense, he tended to side with the more conservative planters. He didn't care for Patrick Henry, as I recall, but occasionally he would side with those who thought that Parliament was going too far—he opposed the Stamp Act and eventually supported the resolutions of the Committee on Correspondence. I can't see anyone killing him for those views."

"Nor I," said Norvell. "What did you know about his financial situation? Had he ever approached you for financial help? Apparently he was in some financial difficulty."

"Yes, I had heard that he was in some difficulty. But no, he did not come to me for financial assistance. Not that I could have helped him anyway," said Chiswell. "With the price of tobacco where it is, we all are living on thin margins."

"Who else might he have approached?" asked Norvell. "I understand that sometimes Speaker Robinson helped out some of the planters with loans."

"Well you would have to speak to the Speaker about that," said Chiswell. "He never said anything to me about lending money to Mr. Johnson, or about Johnson approaching him. I doubt it, but you need to ask him."

Norvell told Chiswell that Speaker Robinson also had denied loaning Mr. Johnson any money, and he thanked him for his time and answers. As he was leaving, Norvell asked Chiswell if he could think of any reason why Johnson would be meeting someone at the Powder Magazine at midnight. "It does not make any sense to me," said Chiswell.

The Sheriff also was able to find James Johnson's friend John Page, a delegate from Gloucester. The two men were not close, but had seen each other at various social events in Williamsburg. "I know you have spoken with George Wythe about the investigation into the death of your friend James Johnson; however, I have a few more questions if you have the time for me?"

"Of course, Sheriff," said Page. "What can I tell you that I haven't told Mr. Wythe? I am very sorry about James. He was a true friend, probably my best friend other than Tom Jefferson."

"Two mysteries you might help me to unravel," said Norvell. "You had told Mrs. George that you were leaving on Sunday and yet apparently stayed for dinner at Chowning's and later met with Tom Jefferson and didn't actually leave until Monday."

"Let me clear that up first," said Page. "I had wanted to meet with Tom before I left town and he was away until the evening, so I had dinner at Chowning's and met with Tom about eleven in the evening at his place. I know that seems unusual, but I had some news to share. I was headed to Robert Burwell's plantation to ask his daughter Frances to marry me. I had high hopes in the success of that venture and so wanted to celebrate in advance with my closest friend. I was fortunate and am now engaged to marry Frances."

"Congratulations!" said Norvell. "That certainly clears up the mystery in a most respectable manner. I can now understand the bit of secrecy involved. Did James Johnson also know of the possible engagement?"

"No, I wanted to make sure of the acceptance before telling him and he did seem a bit pre-occupied—I suppose about the financial issues that were mentioned at the inquest," said Page.

"To me, that is the second mystery," said Norvell. "If Mr. Johnson was in financial difficulty, I would have thought that he might have gone to you to see if you could help. Did he do that?"

"Yes, he did discuss his financial difficulties with me," said Page. "Of course I would have been glad to help if that was possible. But my father left most of the estate to my brother Mann Page III and my legacy is very much tied up with the plantation. Like so many planters, we have been hit hard by the value of sterling relative to tobacco, so we are among those who are land rich and cash poor. We have had to negotiate extensions of our own notes to our bankers in England and Scotland."

"James understood I was not in a position to help him at this time," continued Page, "however, he seemed more confident recently that he had found a possible solution. But he did not confide in me as to what that was. I wish I could assist you more. I do want you to find out who murdered him and why. It is a mystery to me."

Norvell thanked Mr. Page and said he might have further questions for him. Page indicated he would be happy to assist as needed.

CHAPTER 15

George Wythe had invited Sheriff Norvell and Luck Key to dinner at his home that afternoon, in part because he was interested in how the case was progressing. It also gave Key and Norvell a chance to relate what they had learned during the day.

Sheriff Norvell had not been to the Wythe house before and so was given a tour of the house and gardens. The private garden between the kitchen garden and work yard was lovely. A shell covered path led along a well-manicured, pleached hornbeam arbor, a method of training trees to produce a narrow screen or hedge by tying in and interlacing vines along a supporting framework to provide a pleasant symmetry and some privacy. A wood bench at the end allowed one to sit and relax, read or reflect on the day's events.

The kitchen garden included an area for herbs and vegetables, while the "pleasure" garden contained a mixture of wild and planted flowers, tulips from Holland, roses and others. A variety of outbuildings included stables, a dovecote for housing pigeons, a chicken coup and the kitchen, located just behind the house. There were a variety of other out buildings including a laundry, housing for the servants, and the "necessary." It was quite a large complex, especially located in town, just paces from the Governor's Palace.

The house itself was a two story brick structure and small attic, sitting on a raised basement. Mr. Wythe told Norvell that the house was originally built by the architect Richard Taliaferro for himself, but was given to Wythe upon his marriage to Elizabeth Taliaferro. The first floor contained a large foyer, with wood stairs leading to the upper level. In the front of the house were the parlor on one side of the hall and dining room on the other. In the back was Wythe's study, which he used for his law offices, and a large library just opposite. Mr. Wythe said the four family bedrooms were upstairs, two on each side, including one used by his wife for her study and crafts.

Norvell was impressed with both the house itself and with the attached gardens that were clearly the pride and joy of Mr. Wythe. "My wife thinks it is a question whether I like books more than flowers," said Wythe. "I ascribe to Cicero's views that if you have a garden and a library, you have everything you need! Of course, I would amend that to include my lovely wife Elizabeth."

"Now to the business at hand. What have you learned so far?" asked Wythe.

Luck went first, describing his meetings with merchants and the interview with Jacob. "Of course, Jacob could still be guilty," said Key. "He does have a motive and no alibi. He could have made up the story about the Roan horse tied up near the Powder Magazine, in order to shift the blame elsewhere. There is no other witness to that fact. And he did not mention it at the first interview with him. Still, I am inclined to believe Jacob. He also mentioned that Mr. Johnson and Mr. Mechem may have had their differences, especially as to the treatment of the Negroes and that Mr. Johnson's financial troubles seemed to increase after Mr. Mechem became the overseer."

"I guess the question about Jacob," said Wythe, "is why Mr. Johnson would be willing to meet with him at Midnight at the Powder Magazine? Johnson would have known that Jacob might still be angry, even with his rather good position with the blacksmith. What would Mr. Johnson, or Jacob for that matter, have to gain by such a meeting? That is what makes so little sense to me. Though I still cannot see why Mr. Johnson would make such a meeting with anyone."

"Well, I think he still stands out as a possible, if not likely, suspect," said Norvell. "Luck your information on Mr. Mechem adds to our rather negative impression of him. But why would Mechem come to Williamsburg to kill Mr. Johnson, unless he was trying to shift the blame to Jacob? I think we will need to have some further discussions with him at some point."

Sheriff Norvell then discussed his interviews at the Capitol. He clarified the questions about John Page and said he assumed that Tom Jefferson would provide whatever alibi Page needed. Without naming Henry Lee, he indicated that there were some questions by members of the House about the loans that Speaker John Robinson provided to some of the planters. Speaker Robinson was considered one of Virginia's richest men but lending out to fellow plantation owners was unusual.

"There appears to be some concern that the funds loaned out were not all from the Speaker's private estate," said Norvell. "There is an ongoing investigation concerning the operations of the Treasury. Apparently a 1762 report from a House of Burgesses Committee found nothing wrong. However, there is now a new investigation underway. Exactly how this might fit in with the murder of James Johnson remains a mystery to me. Anyone have any opinions on that?"

George Wythe thoughtfully reviewed his own position and thinking. He was a beneficiary of a small loan from Robinson, which at the time seemed no issue, though he had not yet repaid the loan. "I suppose," said Wythe carefully, "that if all of the funds were not Speaker Robinson's, there might be some embarrassment, both to the Speaker and to those that bor-rowed funds from him. Though again, is that a motive for mur-der? Certainly Robinson, at his current age and state of health, could not have wielded the murder weapon. And it is hard to believe that anyone else would take such action."

"And how was all of this supposed to benefit Mr. Johnson?" asked Norvell.

"John Mechem, Mr. Johnson's overseer, indicated that he thought Johnson intended to meet with someone that might provide some financial assistance—although again we only have Mechem's word for that," observed Key. "My impression is that Mr. Johnson was not close to the Speaker, so maybe he was meeting with someone that could petition the Speaker on his behalf. His colleague, Carter Braxton, for example. That would be the logical person. James Johnson was Braxton's neighbor, they both represented King William County in the House. He would be the person that makes the most sense."

"Braxton did not exactly deny that he tried to facilitate a loan from the Speaker to Johnson," said Norvell. "I will have to go back and address that question to him directly. Mr. Key, what were your notes about the people at Chowning's?"

"Mr. Chowning said that he didn't remember or know all of the people that were there on Sunday night," said Key. "However, he mentioned that he thought three members of the House of Burgesses were there, Edmund Chiswell, John Page and Richard Adams. He specifically said he didn't recognize everyone but assumed most were here for business with the legislature or Governor,"

"That is interesting, and perhaps we shall have to have further discussions with the three gentlemen, although I think we can now rule out Mr. Page," said Norvell. "I did speak with Mr. Chiswell earlier today. His sister is the third and current wife of Speaker Robinson and I gather that perhaps he has some influence on the Speaker's financial dealings. However, he denied being close to Mr. Johnson and he said that he was not involved in any financial loans from Speaker Robinson to members of the House of Burgesses."

"I don't need to tell you how to do your job," Mr. Wythe said to Norvell. "But you are treading on some very sensitive issues of powerful people. You certainly need to have much more evidence than at present to place anyone at the Powder Magazine the night of the murder."

Norvell acknowledged the truth of that statement. "Yes," he said. "It would be much more convenient if we arrested Jacob for the murder and didn't rock any political boats. But my job is to find the truth about this murder, wherever the evidence takes me, even if I step on some toes. I guess I feel I have some political capital and won't be thrown under the cart." He paused. "Still, you are right. We need a lot more to go on before we go charging in to accuse anyone."

Norvell suggested that he and Mr. Key would have to determine where all of the potential actors were on Sunday night and see if anyone had the opportunity, motive, and ability to pull off such a crime. "We will also have to check on whether Mr. Mechem has an alibi for the time of Mr. Johnson's death. He was quick to try to shift the blame to Jacob, maybe he was trying to divert the attention from his own possible actions."

He then asked Mr. Wythe about the rumors he was hearing about possible action against the Stamp Act in the House of Burgesses. Mr. Wythe explained the status as he was aware of it. "In an effort to raise funds to pay off debts and defend the vast new American territories won from the French in the Seven Years' War, from 1756 to 1763, the British Parliament adopted the Stamp Act over protests from the colonies. The legislation levies a direct tax on all materials printed for commercial and legal use in the colonies, from newspapers and pamphlets to playing cards and dice."

Wythe noted that Stamp Acts were a common fund-raising vehicle in England, but the colonists had recently been hit with two other major taxes: the Sugar Act in 1764, which levied new duties on imports of textiles, wines, coffee and sugar; and the Currency Act in 1764, which caused a major decline in the value of the paper money used by colonists. While most Virginians did not like these two actions, there was a general recognition of Parliament's ability to regulate commercial interests in England and the colonies.

"The Stamp Act, however," said Wythe "is regarded as something different. It is a direct tax on domestic activities that Parliament had avoided in the past. Virginians and other colonial legislatures see this as an issue of direct taxation without representation in Parliament. Until this potential measure

Virginia and other colonies have been allowed by Parliament to decide which taxes would be imposed and collected."

"Last year I drafted for the Committee on Correspondence a strongly worded statement indicating our opposition to this measure," said Wythe. "The 'Remonstrances of the Council and Burgesses of Virginia' noted that we often adopted taxes as requested by Parliament to fund domestic priorities and we did not contest Parliament's ability to tax trade. But we noted that it is essential to British liberty that laws imposing taxes on the people ought not to be made without the consent of the representatives chosen by the people. There were examples cited where tax recommendations were made by the Governor for the welfare and good government of the colony had been approved by the Council and Burgesses."

"Further," Wythe continued, "we noted the importance of Virginia's agricultural production to Great Britain and our consumption of their manufacture suppliers, benefiting both parties. We concluded by indicating our strong opposition to what we viewed as the exercise of anti-constitutional power, which would set a dangerous example for the whole British Empire."

"Unfortunately, Governor Fauquier informed us that Parliament has ignored our messages and passed the new legislation. We have been told by our own sources that our 'Remonstrances' were not even considered by Parliament, let alone debated. Naturally, members of the House of Burgesses are up in arms, and there appears to be a movement to take some more official position in opposition to the measure. This will probably happen on Monday and it might be interesting for the two of you to observe the action. I am not sure whether this political issue has anything to do with the murder of Mr. Johnson, but we may be at an historical watershed here in Virginia," Wythe concluded, "and you both may want to be there to witness the event."

CHAPTER 16

Saturday May 25

Saturday looked like another beautiful day. Key walked the short way to Chowning's to have breakfast with Sheriff Norvell and discuss the next steps of the investigation. Breakfast in the tavern usually consisted of hot corn rolls, jam and chicken or beef. Norvell laid out a course for them for the day. He had some other business that he had to attend to and asked Luck to check around at the area stables to see if any one recognized the description of the horse that Jacob had claimed to see the night of the murder. "Even if not one-hundred percent certain," said Norvell, "I think we have to assume that Jacob did see a horse, possibly a Roan. It is our only real lead at this point."

"Take the afternoon off and I will plan on stopping by early tomorrow at the Wythe house to pick you up for the ride to the Johnson plantation. We won't be in the same rush as last time, so I would expect it to take us about 5 hours to get to their plantation. While this is a social event, we do not want to neglect the opportunity to further examine possibilities with respect to the murder of Mr. Johnson. We also should check on Mr. Mechem's alibi at the time of the murder."

Luck set out to visit the stables in the area. He decided to walk, so he could enjoy the nice day and explore a little of Williamsburg on foot. He had never seen anything like the beautiful houses and gardens in the city. He imagined other cities might impress him as well, though he had not been outside of Virginia, so his knowledge was limited. He didn't think that Jamestown was on the same level as Williamsburg, nor the small towns in Louisa County, where he was from.

The first stable visited was George Wythe's, just behind the house complex. A large barn contained a fine carriage and stalls for four horses. A paddock area adjacent allowed the horses to roam and graze. One of Wythe's servants, Sam, showed him around. Wythe's four horses were Cleveland Bays, a well-established breed in Virginia, named for the Cleveland region of Yorkshire, England. The horses are tall, but not extremely so, and are quite beautiful. The reddish-brown color of their bodies are set against black legs. Sam noted that the most distinguishing feature of the horses are their feet, which are wider than other horses and very sturdy, allowing them to be used for a variety of purposes from individual riding to pulling a carriage.

Luck had already ridden one of the horses on his ride the previous Monday to find the Sheriff and later to ride to the Johnson Plantation. He had not had an opportunity to do a lot of horseback riding, but enjoyed being on a fast horse, even though he was fairly sore after that first full day of riding. Sam said he was not aware of any Roan horses in Williamsburg, but there always were lots of visitors during the sessions of the House of Burgesses, so a Roan could easily have been ridden by one of the visitors.

Next Luck went a half block to the Robert Carter house, a lovely two-story wood home with a portico over a central entrance. Shuttered windows graced both sides of the entrance, with three large windows on the second floor. On either side were covered walkways to the various out buildings, including the kitchen and stables. George Wythe had told him that Mr. Carter owned a substantial plantation in Virginia, but was often in Williamsburg because of his duties on the Governor's Council. He walked up the few steps to the front door and knocked. Nearly immediately an older Negro man answered the door and asked Luck what his business was with Mr. Carter. Luck explained that he was working for Sheriff Norvell and wanted to talk to someone from the stables about a matter that related to the murder of James Johnson.

From inside, Luck heard a man call out, "Mr. Daniel, who is there?" Daniel asked Luck to come into the home and to the right was a parlor where visitors were received. A man Luck assumed to be Robert Carter entered and Luck introduced himself and gave a short version of his role in assisting Sheriff Norvell on the murder of Mr. Johnson.

"I know Norvell well," said Carter, "and I am pleased to provide you any information that you might need." Luck explained the sighting of the Roan horse. "I have seen only one Roan horse recently, which I thought might belong to the silversmith James Craig, however my groomsman may have more knowledge on this subject than I do. Mr. Daniel, will you please show Mr. Key through the house and find Mr. Thomas to see if he knows anything."

Thanking Mr. Carter, Luck went with Daniel to talk to Thomas. While walking to the stable area Luck told Daniel that he was interested in Mr. Carter's salutation to him as Mr. Daniel, not something most slave owners do.

"Well, Mr. Carter freed me and my wife Ruth who is his longtime housekeeper. He now pays us a salary and treats us as he does any other worker."

Luck was quite amazed at this information. "Was there a particular reason for his actions?" asked Key.

"Mr. Carter is a great man and after we had worked for him as slaves for a number of years, he said that we deserved our freedom. He is a religious man and does not believe in slavery. In fact, all of his servants in Williamsburg are free Negroes and he pays us wages. He doesn't make a big deal of it because other slave owners might not approve and there is a current legal issue concerning the freeing or manumission of slaves in Virginia."

Daniel showed Luck around the house and its structures, which followed an unusual plan for Williamsburg, with the most elaborate entertaining room at the rear, facing a broad garden. Its location of windows also responded to this orientation, with just three bays of doors and windows across the Palace Green side and five bays across its rear. The views from the rear rooms took in a terraced garden, and were unobstructed by the customary collection of domestic work and service buildings including the stables, as these were all set to the sides of the main house. Luck commented on the beautiful symmetry of the design. "Here is Thomas now," said Daniel.

After Daniel had explained to Thomas who Luck was and the purpose of the visit, Luck asked if Thomas had seen a Roan horse recently in Williamsburg. After some thought, Thomas said that he was aware of a few Roan horses in Williamsburg. "I think one may be owned by the silversmith James Craig," said Thomas. "And I do remember seeing a beautiful dark Roan horse one day near the Capitol Building, but I could not give you any information about who the horse might belong to. Roans are quite rare in Williamsburg, but of course it is not as if I was gathering information about them. Mr. Carter actually owns a light-colored Roan horse, but we do not bring her to Williamsburg from the Nomony plantation. I am sorry I can't help you more."

Luck thanked Daniel and Thomas for their information and thought about what he had learned so far. There were some Roan horses owned either by residents or visitors to Williamsburg, but not so many. That enhanced their chances of finding the one Roan horse that Jacob said he had seen near the Powder Magazine. He also thought about what he had just learned. He knew there were free Negroes in Virginia, but he had not had any contact with one until he met Daniel and Thomas. What was his own thinking about slavery? Even though his parents had owned no slaves, he assumed that was simply because they did not have the finances to purchase one. But maybe, like Robert Carter, they were uneasy with the moral dimensions. Is it right for one person to 'own' another? He would have to find time to talk this over with Mr. Wythe and Sheriff Norvell.

Luck walked over to the Governor's Palace and, after an explanation to the Governor's butler of why he was there, was allowed to speak to the coachmen and grooms at the Governor's stables. The Governor has a large stage house with two coaches, the larger one pulled by six horses. Again, no one remembered seeing a Roan horse, which meant the person with a Roan horse was not likely a regular visitor at the Governor's Palace or the grooms would have taken care of the horse. That would seem to support Thomas' story that Mr. Carter did not bring his Roan to Williamsburg or they would have likely seen it.

Luck walked south from the Governor's Palace along the Palace Green and turned left at Nicholson Street, walking one block to where Peyton Randolph's large house stood. Mr. Randolph was one of the more influential members of the House of Burgesses, perhaps second only to Speaker Robinson and he was widely respected. His house was somewhat larger than George Wythe's house but constructed of wood instead of brick, the entrance set in the center bay, sheltered by a gabled roof. Rather than bother the family, Key went around to the back area that contained a number of outbuildings, including a stable. He found one of the Randolph's groomsmen and asked about whether he had seen a Roan horse here in Williamsburg.

"I don't know sir," said James. "Mr. Randolph has a lot of visitors, especially during the sessions of the House of Burgesses. Can you tell me what a Roan horse looks like?"

"Well, there are a lot of different colors of Roan horses, but the one described to me might have been a "blue" Roan, with generally dark, possibly black, hair with white or silver hair interspersed, so I guess it would be a mixed color, because of the black and white hair," said Key. "And the head and legs tend to be a solid color, such as black."

"I do remember one such horse," said James. "I think it may have belonged to Speaker Robinson or a friend of his. I know that I took care of a horse as you described last month. I don't remember if it was Mr. Robinson's, or perhaps someone that came with him. It was a beauty with black and white hair over the body and all black on his legs and main. You will have to ask Mr. Randolph or Speaker Robinson about it as I can't tell you anymore."

This was certainly an interesting development thought Key on leaving the stable area. Of course, he was not in a position to question either Mr. Randolph or Speaker Robinson. That task would have to be left to the Sheriff.

Luck spent the next few hours visiting each of the stables in the Williamsburg area. They were mostly off the main streets so he took each of the side streets off of Nicholson and Francis Streets to see what stables existed. He did find one other stable that offered some possibilities. It was tucked behind the Public Goal just off of Nicholson Street. The owner said that he had seen a Roan horse, such as the one described, but could not remember whose it was.

He actually was stabling a Roan horse for the silversmith, James Craig, just as Robert Carter recalled. It was a dark brown horse with white hair that gave the horse a chocolate look. Quite lovely and possibly in the dark might have been the horse that Jacob claimed to see. But that opened up the question of why the silversmith would tie up the horse on Francis Street near the Powder Magazine, when he could just have easily had the horse in its stables and walked to the Magazine if he was meeting Johnson there.

Key stopped by Craig's Silversmith Shop on the way back to the Wythe house. Unfortunately, Craig was not in. Some of his apprentices where working on a variety of silver pieces, including jewelry and cutlery. He was quite struck with the workmanship of the silver. The prices were substantial and he could see how Craig could easily afford his beautiful Roan horse.

* * *

That afternoon Luck joined Mr. Wythe in the library, where Wythe often did his work and reading when he was not entertaining clients in his study. "Mr. Wythe, may I ask you a question?" asked Key.

"Of course," Wythe replied, "and I am interested in knowing

how you are finding your current position with Sheriff Norvell."

Everything was happening so quickly that Luck had to sort out his own thoughts before responding. Wythe was such a gentle man and yet the brightest person that Key had ever met. At times Luck felt like he was looking at his situation as if it was happening to someone else and not to him—it was so different than anything he had experienced. He very much wanted to please Mr. Wythe and hoped that this relationship would continue to develop.

"I like Sheriff Norvell," said Key. "I find he has a very logical mind and is good at sorting out facts. He listens to what people are saying and doesn't try to use his office to bully people. I guess I have seen that happen before, so his restraint and modesty is something that I have come to appreciate."

"Good!" said Wythe. "Now ask me your question and I will try to provide you an answer."

"Well," Key hesitated and was somewhat embarrassed. "I have been here for less than a week and so much has opened up for me. I am greatly appreciative of your hiring me as a junior clerk and for the opportunity to work with the Sheriff and to meet Thomas Jefferson. My background is modest. My father was a farmer and we always had the basics, but I am not sure that is a life I want to lead. I could take my modest inheritance and buy land to farm, but I would like something more in life. I don't really know what at this point. So I am hoping that you can provide me with some ideas and a possible path that would open up other avenues and prospects."

George Wythe thought for a moment. "Look around you. What do you see?"

"You have a marvelous library. I don't think I have ever seen as many books in one place as you have in this room," Key answered.

"Don't think of these as books," said Wythe. "Think of them as knowledge and ideas to be gathered and stored for future use, just as animals store food for the winter."

"You might be surprised at my own modest upbringing," continued Wythe. "My mother Margaret tutored me as I was growing up. I was fortunate that she came from a Quaker background whose followers believed, as I do, that women should be educated just as men, so she was quite accomplished herself. Our Plantation life was a constant struggle and she might have limited me and my siblings' education to math and English— enough to get by in rural Virginia. Instead she found books in Latin and Greek and instilled in us a love for the classics and a love of learning. I only had one year of college, as we could not afford the tuition. However, I began to read a great deal from a variety of books and eventually decided to study law, which I did on my own and eventually at another law office. I was only 20 when I was admitted to the Virginia Bar. As I became more financially independent, I began to collect books for my library. These are not decorations to impress others, but knowledge that I can gather and husband for use later."

"So my first advice to you is to continually develop yourself," said Wythe.

"You have my permission to access any of my books. Plan to read something new every day. I know you are tired at night, but don't go to sleep without some reading. It will become a habit and will allow you to learn more, about the world, about yourself and about others. Yes, it would be nice to go to college, but you have a college-level library here close to your door. You just need to have the motivation to use it." Luck nodded affirmatively.

"My second advice is to not worry too much about the future. You are still very young; enjoy and acquire knowledge from your present positions. Watch and learn from the behavior of others. You have already noted some aspects of Sheriff Norvell's leadership ability that you like. You will find that there are many leadership styles and approaches to human interaction. Think of other people. How are they treated? Are they demeaned or enhanced? You always want to be an enhancer!"

"My last piece of advice is a question of character." said

Wythe. "Your integrity is something you must protect. Be humble, as you will not know all of the answers. Cicero said that humility is the solid foundation for all virtues and I would agree. Be diligent in asking others for advice. Don't try to show someone up by acting like you know more than they do. Use Norvell's approach of listening. If you do this you will find that others will value your opinions more and that your reputation will gradually grow. In the final analysis, your character and your reputation will lead to other opportunities."

"Aristotle observed that good character and achieving excellence are not individual acts, but years of habit—what you do continually. Your habits then become part of you and you don't need to think about what is right or wrong in any situation. Well, I hope that was not too long-winded an answer," said Wythe. "Start by looking at my library. What is here that interests you?"

Wythe showed Key around the library noting the various sections and books contained in each. It was an interesting variety of leather-bound books and mostly not about the law. Of course there were a lot of law cases, chancery reports, minutes of Parliament as well as books by Blackstone, Jacob, Nelson, Danvers, and others. Wythe also had a number of books of history and philosophy, including the Bible and books by Bacon, Caesar, Cicero, Hobbes, Locke, Machiavelli, Plutarch and Plato. Literature included Homer's Odyssey and Iliad, Shakespeare and Milton. There were books on mathematics, science and agriculture. There were so many books, perhaps over 300, that Key was overwhelmed.

"I suggest you pick something that is entertaining and educational. Perhaps one of Shakespeare's plays would be a good start," said Wythe. "His histories generally follow real events and you cannot gain a better understanding of people and their motivations than by reading Shakespeare!"

Key took the copy of one of the books in the eight volume *The Works of Shakespeare* and noticed that the volume contained the play *Henry V*. "One of my favorite plays," said Wythe. "And a good place to start."

Luck thanked Mr. Wythe both for his advice and for the use of his library. He looked forward to reading *Henry V* and other books so that perhaps he would be better prepared to understand and participate in the important discussions of the day.

＊ ＊ ＊

That night George had his daily discussion with Elizabeth. "This case really bothers me. I am worried that we will find out that the murderer is someone we know. What else explains why Johnson would meet someone late at night? He must have known James Johnson and so it is likely that we know the person too, possibly a merchant or a member of the House of Burgesses. It is hard for me to think why someone would kill James. I guess it is possible that the murderer was his former slave Jacob or someone Johnson knew from his plantation or other work; but a murder in Williamsburg? I think it points to someone we know."

"George, not everyone we know is a friend. If the evidence points to someone, we'll just have to see how the facts develop. Perhaps you are jumping out ahead of the evidence. The Sheriff seems a fine man. After all, this is his investigation, not yours, even if you have become involved because of finding the body and your new relationship with young Mr. Key," said Elizabeth. "I heard you giving the young man a lecture about his future."

"Well not really a lecture," demurred George. "He did ask for my advice and you know I always have plenty of that! But you are right, as usual, about the investigation. I have been asked to help and that is all I can do. William will do a good job, I am sure of that. I just hope we don't uncover something that would be damaging to any of our friends here in Williamsburg. It would be nice if the murderer was outside our orbit of friends and acquaintances. But enough of that for tonight. I noticed that you were reading when I came in. What book did you pick up this time? Could it be Shakespeare? I noticed one of the volumes was missing when Mr. Key selected his reading."

"You guessed it," said Elizabeth, "although I was more interested in reading something a bit lighter than his histories or tragedies. I am again reading his sonnets. They are so beautiful and I remember when you first read those to me just after our marriage. I loved you for that and for everything we have been through together. Now I suggest we get some sleep. Tomorrow is Sunday, maybe we can have an outing somewhere if the weather is nice."

"Yes, let's do that. Perhaps a carriage ride to the James River and a lunch," said George. "What a fabulous idea and we can put this whole murder investigation behind us for a day."

CHAPTER 17

Sunday May 26

When Luck arose early on Sunday morning, the sun was not yet up. He washed and dressed in his best clothes, conscious that he did not really own the clothes of a gentleman, more of a servant or worker. But it was the best he could do.

When he went downstairs, to his surprise, a small breakfast had been prepared for him, he supposed by the housekeeper Liddy. And on one chair was a red silk and wool waistcoat. A note next to it was from Thomas Jefferson: "Please accept this gift; it is too small for me now and should fit you. I thought you should have something nice to wear for your Sunday dinner outing. Best wishes, Tom."

How thoughtful, Luck mused. It was a beautiful waistcoat and a very nice gesture from someone whom he had barely met. He wondered whether George Wythe had said something to Jefferson. Regardless, now he did not feel so under-dressed.

Sheriff William Norvell arrived promptly at seven, with the sun just rising and they set off for the Johnson Plantation; the journey would take most of the morning. Luck observed that the Sheriff had dressed up somewhat from his more austere clothing. He had on black britches and silk stockings, brightly shined shoes with a silver buckle, a blue silk waistcoat and a black flock overcoat. Luck thought this is what a prosperous gentlemen should look like. He knew that dress did not make the person, but the way a person dressed did signal to others your general status in society. Right or wrong, that is just how people felt.

On the way to the plantation, Luck informed Sheriff Norvell of his investigations into the Roan horse. "Interesting," said Norvell. "Can you remind me of the people that were at Clowning's the night of the murder?"

Luck took out his note pad from his pocket. "The three members of the House of Burgesses there were Edmund Chiswell, John Page and Richard Adams. Of course there were other people too, who were not as well known to the owner."

"Mr. Chiswell is Speaker Robinson's brother-in-law," said Norvell, "so it is possible that he may have been with Robinson when he was at Randolph's house and may be the owner of the Roan horse seen by Jacob. That is certainly something we will have to follow as a possible lead. Silversmith Craig's involvement seems less likely. As you pointed out, he could have easily left his horse in his stables and walked to the Powder Magazine. Still, I will ask you to talk with him on Tuesday. And I know the Roan horse of Robert Carter. He does keep it at his plantation and I have never seen it in Williamsburg. Of course our inquiry is contingent on whether Jacob did see a horse tied up near the Magazine and whether it was a Roan horse that he saw in the dark. However, this is our only lead and I think it is most important that we pursue it to whatever conclusion it leads."

They arrived at the Johnson Plantation about noon and were met by the Johnson butler, Samuel, who had another servant take care of the horses. Samuel showed the two gentlemen into the parlor. They were shortly thereafter greeted by Sarah Johnson.

Sarah wore a black dress, with long black sleeves and a high collar with a fringe of white around her neck. She asked them if they would like some refreshments after their long ride. They said yes and she suggested lemonade, freshly squeezed from a lemon tree in their garden.

"I know that lemons are used in Virginia primarily for decorations and medicine," said Mrs. Johnson, "but I have learned a new recipe to create a refreshing drink—a combination of lemon juice, cold water, sugar and often fresh mint or other garnish. My husband believed that the drink originated in Egypt and I have concocted my own formula. Would you like to try some?" They enthusiastically agreed to the offer and Mrs. Johnson asked Samuel to bring some in from the kitchen.

While waiting, Sarah Johnson thanked Sheriff Norvell for arranging for her husband's remains to be returned to the plantation. "We had a nice simple ceremony yesterday," Sarah said, "and we buried James on the hill overlooking the plantation under a large Hickory tree that he so loved. Please tell me what we owe you or the coroner for arranging for his remains to be brought here." Sheriff Norvell said nothing was owed, it was taken care of by the county. Sarah was uncertain whether to believe this or not, but again thanked the Sheriff for making the arrangements.

As Samuel came back from the kitchen with the drinks, Bethany came into the parlor. They both stood and greeted her. Bethany wore a simple black blouse and skirt in honor of her father. They toasted one another's health and the memory of James Johnson and drank the cool drink. "This is a most refreshing and unusual drink," said Luck. "I have never had anything like it." Norvell agreed and asked how they managed to grow lemon trees. While Virginia winters were not particularly harsh, the occasional low temperatures would make it impossible or very difficult for lemon trees to survive.

"This was my husband's idea," said Mrs. Johnson. "During his travels he investigated various ways to keep a garden during the winter. George Washington, for example, has constructed a hothouse or greenhouse that provides extra sun and warmth during winter months and a few other plantation owners in the area also have greenhouses. Our greenhouse allows us to grow the lemons and certain flowers and vegetables year round."

"I admit to having not seen one," said the Sheriff. "Perhaps if time permits you can show it to me." Mrs. Johnson indicated that she would be glad to do so.

"We are planning dinner for about two o'clock," said Mrs. Johnson. "Bethany, why don't you show Mr. Key around the house grounds. I have a few things I would like to discuss with the Sheriff." Bethany and Luck agreed and they walked out of the parlor and through the back door to the gardens behind the house.

"Well I am glad to have you to myself," said Bethany. Luck turned a bit red and returned the compliment, suggesting that she call him Luck. "And please call me Bethany. I am at an awkward age when I am not yet a women, but not a child, so I don't really like being called Miss Johnson or Miss Bethany—just Bethany is fine. Luck is such an unusual name; what is the story of the name, if I am not being too personal?"

"I wish I knew for sure," said Luck. "My parents told me that mother had difficulties with my birth and that I was lucky to have survived. But I also know there was another family in a neighboring county whose surname was Luck, so perhaps that is the reason. I do get kidded about the name."

They walked through the gardens and grounds that were not as extensive as at the Wythe house but still quite lovely. There was a substantial kitchen garden with herbs and vegetables and Luck saw a couple of lemon trees in large wooden containers, the source of their wonderful drink. The private garden was laid out as a maze lined with rose bushes that one walked through and eventually entered a small private space with a couple of benches and an apple tree. They sat down on one of the benches.

"Your mother must love roses," said Luck. "They are most beautiful here and I am sure take quite a bit of work. It is fortunate that you have help to take care of them." He saw Bethany start to tear-up and asked her if he had said something to offend her.

"No," said Bethany. "It is just that both my father and mother loved the roses and he took a special pride in keeping them up, often by personally instructing the servants on their care, and my father even did some pruning himself. Mother seems to have lost interest in the roses since my father's death and I am not sure we will even be able to keep the servants to take care of them. Maybe that will have to be something that I will do myself."

"I hope you can keep them up," said Luck. "This really is a special place. It must be nice to come here and read or just sit and relax." Luck thought how fortunate he was to be here with this beautiful young girl even if thoughts of a future relationship seemed a distant dream. "I wish there was something I could do to assist you."

"How did you come to work for Sheriff Norvell?" Bethany asked. "I know you are a long way from here, living in Williamsburg, but maybe you could come out occasionally on the weekend if the Sheriff gave you the time off. I would like that very much."

Luck felt that he would like that as well, though he did not know how practical it was. "I am actually the junior clerk for Mr. George Wythe," he said. "Sheriff Norvell's under-sheriff is in London and he asked Mr. Wythe if he could 'borrow' me for the investigation. I don't know how long this will last or how busy I will be for Mr. Wythe. It is a great opportunity for me to work with both of these gentlemen. When my long-range duties with Mr. Wythe are spelled out, I hope that I might have some weekends off and could make the trip out here to see and support you in any way I can." Luck wanted it very much to be true.

In the house, Sarah Johnson was discussing the case with Sheriff Norvell. He updated her on the investigation and said they were making some progress, though he could not say how long it would take to complete or if they will have a final answer to all of the mystery.

"Mrs. Johnson" said Norvell. "Please call me Sarah," she replied, "I feel we can be on first name basis now." Sheriff Norvell asked her to call him William. "Is there anything that I can do to assist you in this difficult situation?" he said.

"William," asked Sarah, "would it be possible for you to do

me a favor, if I am not asking too much." William said for her to please ask. "I am frankly overwhelmed by the financial issues facing the plantation. John Mechem has suggested selling some of the land or some more of the slaves. I really don't know what to do, or whether we will be able to hang on to the plantation. My husband and I had no sons that survived and so in his will he has left the plantation to Bethany, when she comes of age, with a lifetime benefit to myself. Of course, he was in good health and no one anticipated his death at an early age.

"There also are some legal issues in the will that I need to clarify," she said "for example, what happens if we have to sell the plantation? It is all just so overwhelming right now, I just don't know what we will do." Sarah began to quietly cry and William came over and put his arms around her to comfort her.

"I wish that I was closer to you than Williamsburg," said William. "But what I can do, as soon as this investigation is over, is sit down with Mr. Mechem and more thoroughly go through the options and try to get a picture of the financial future of the plantation. You know that most of the plantation owners have financial problems now so you are not alone in your worries. I cannot promise you that I will find a successful option, but I do promise to try my best and to look at every possible solution. Try not to take any action that is irreversible."

Norvell also suggested to her that she consult with George Wythe on any legal matters. "No one is better regarded than Mr. Wythe. I am sure he could handle any issue that arises in a discrete manner."

"What is your thinking about Mr. Mechem," asked William. "Can you trust him? Is it possible that he had a falling out with your husband that might have precipitated some conflict between the two? If you are uncomfortable with Mechem, I can help you find another overseer."

"I know that James had increasing concerns about Mr. Mechem's management. He treated the slaves much more harshly than our previous overseer and James was often very upset about it. If you are wondering whether Mr. Mechem is a possible suspect in the murder, I can't say for sure whether he might have left the plantation last Sunday for Williamsburg. That would be a long trip there and back. He was here on Monday morning," said Sarah. Norvell thought it unlikely that Mechem could have made that round trip ride without someone noticing, but thought he would have to check that out.

"William, it is very kind of you to help us understand the financial issues we are facing," Sarah said with some emotion. "I just feel adrift now." Sarah looked up at William and the two locked eyes for a moment, each with their own thoughts. Sarah thought William was very handsome and sympathetic. However, she had just lost a husband she loved and would not let her thoughts drift to another man. William thought Sarah was quite striking. She had a dignity and calm that he valued and thought how fortunate James Johnson was to have had such a wife. His own wife died some time ago and he had not given a lot of thought to a future with a new wife. But he could see something in Sarah Johnson that he admired and felt he could love her with time, even if this was not the best time for either of them.

"It is almost dinner time," said Sarah. "I think we had better find the youngsters and bring them in. I detect a bit of a spark between them, but Bethany will just turn sixteen next week and is too young to get involved with anyone, especially at this present time. I will be relying on her to assist me if we are going to save this plantation. Still, I have to say that I like Mr. Key."

Just at Sarah and William were getting up to find Bethany and Luck, the two came through the back door. "Your garden is one of the most beautiful that I have seen," said Luck. "The maze of roses surely must be unique."

"Thank you," said Sarah. "They were a project of my husband's and he put a great deal of time in seeing that everything was just right. And I love them; but they take a great deal of work and I am not sure we will be able to keep them up as well as we have in the past." Sarah sighed.

"Oh I hope they do not go to ruin," said Luck. "Bethany said that she would care for them and I promise that I will find the time to come here and help as well. It would be a shame to lose that lovely place."

"Sarah," said William, "you will have to show them to me before we leave. Gardens are a joy, but like anything worthwhile they do take work." They went into the dining room and places had been set for the four of them.

"Everything looks lovely," said William admiring the table place setting and flowers in the middle, presumably from their garden.

They took their places and Samuel began to serve the meal. They started out with crayfish soup, a Virginia specialty, followed by roast pork garnished with herbs and spices, small potatoes, broccoli polonaise, and for dessert a chocolate mousse. Luck thought he had never had such wonderful food and both he and Norvell complemented Sarah and her cook.

"Cuffee is a wonderful cook," said Sarah, "and many of the other plantation owners would love to have a chance to have her work for them."

The talk at the table was relaxed and informal—news from Williamsburg, new items brought in by the ship *Hope,* and thoughts about the upcoming debate over the Stamp Act. While the three deferred to Sheriff Norvell some of the time, both Luck and Bethany shared their own views, as did Sarah. "I wonder whether we will ever be more than vassals of our English overlords?" she asked.

"We are not exactly vassals, even if sometimes it feels that way," said William, "The relationship is complex. We provide goods, tobacco and other items, in exchange for English manufactured items and capital to operate our plantations. So both parties benefit, though I do feel we are taken advantage of at times."

After dinner they adjourned to the parlor for brandy, for the men, and lemonade, for the women. William had noticed a harpsichord and asked Sarah and Bethany if either or both played. "We both play," said Bethany, "though my mother is the far better performer. I do like to accompany her by singing sometimes. Would you like to hear something?"

Both Luck and William enthusiastically supported the idea and, after some persuasion, Sarah sat down at the harpsichord and played a hymn from the *Palmster*, a compilation of songs based on Biblical texts. Both Sarah and Bethany seemed to love singing and as they sang both seemed transposed, out of their mourning and into a better world of faith and hope.

Two encores later, the women indicated that they felt that was enough and as it was getting toward evening, they knew that William and Luck would need to be on their way. Again they offered to put the two men up for the night in a spare bedroom, but William indicated they could not do so as they needed to be in Williamsburg early tomorrow.

Sarah gave William a quick tour of the gardens in the back while Samuel had the horses brought to the front for the gentlemen. Sarah also showed William the greenhouse; it was a square stone building with a hipped or pyramid-shaped roof. It had large windows facing the south. Sarah explained that they kept the lemon trees in large wooded containers and moved them indoors to the greenhouse during the winter months. "The stones retain the winter sun heat, but we have a small stove that we can light on particularly cold winter nights to provide additional heat," said Sarah. "It is a bit of a luxury, I suppose, but we do have fruit and vegetables year around as well as flowers, and most of the cost was in the construction. It does not require a lot of ongoing maintenance."

William was quite impressed with the arrangement and would have liked to have stayed longer but knew he and Luck had to return to Williamsburg. Luck and Bethany said their goodbyes and hoped they would see each other again soon. Before leaving, Sheriff Norvell asked Samuel about Mr. Mechem. "Last Sunday, did you see Mr. Mechem?"

"We are usually free on Sundays and Mr. Mechem does not bother us on that day. The house and field servants usually get together for services and family time. I do not remember seeing Mr. Mechem on Sunday, though that is not unusual. He sometimes has a guest at his cabin on Sunday but I can't recall seeing anyone go there. Would you like me to ask some of the other servants? Or ask our Negro 'driver,' William, who helps Mechem?" asked Samuel.

"Not now," said the Sheriff. "I don't want to increase the tension here on the plantation, nor get you or William out of sorts with Mr. Mechem. For now, please keep this to yourself."

It was a long ride back to Williamsburg and fortunately it was still light for most of the way, although they arrived after ten in the evening. They had not had a lot to say on the way home, each with his own thoughts, but both said what a grand time they had and how delightful to be with two beautiful women. Luck was clearly smitten with Bethany and William thought that there might be a future for him with Sarah. For now, however, it was time to get back to the business at hand—finding the person that murdered James Johnson.

Luck did ask the Sheriff about the term driver that Samuel used. He had not heard that designation before. "On larger plantations," said Norvell, "it is not uncommon to have both a white overseer and a head hand or 'driver,' who often does a lot of the work of an overseer. In fact some smaller plantations cannot afford an overseer and appoint a driver from among the Negro slaves. This often works well and in fact I have been thinking of doing that with my own medium-sized plantation. I don't have that many people and having an overseer adds extra cost that I don't need. Of course, you have to be present more often, or have great confidence in the person you choose. That would be the case for me. My choice for driver has worked for me since he was a boy and probably knows more about running the plantation than I do. I have promised that he will have his freedom upon my death or before, if possible."

"Appointing a driver and ridding herself of Mr. Mechem may be something that Mrs. Johnson should also consider to save money. I do not have good feelings about Mechem; he seems to mistreat the Negroes and possibly impose himself on some of the female Negroes. This is another moral dimension of slavery that troubles me," concluded the Sheriff.

Luck again thought about his own evolving thinking of slavery. In addition to the question of whether it was right for someone to own another person, the treatment and misuse of Negroes was simply not right. Perhaps he had been sheltered from seeing the worst of slavery as William Byers, for whom he had apprenticed, was a mostly benevolent master. George Wythe also treated his Negro slaves with respect and seemed to feel that slavery was an inherent evil. Yet, slavery seemed indispensable to the operations of plantations in Virginia. "Will it ever be possible to find a way out of this dilemma?" Luck pondered.

CHAPTER 18

Monday May 27

George Wythe was in the dining room when Luck came in the next morning. It was later than usual as Luck had been tired from the long trip on Sunday and had difficulties sleeping after the interaction he had with Bethany Johnson. "Well young man," asked Wythe, "how was your Sunday outing? It was a long trip for you and the Sheriff, but I hope it was a rewarding one."

Luck described the day to him, noting that Sarah Johnson told Sheriff Norvell that she was concerned about some legal issues concerning the estate and might consult with Wythe. He was circumspect over the growing feelings that he had for Bethany, and he did not provide any hint as to the Sheriff's possible interest in Mrs. Johnson. He also updated Wythe on the investigation, the search for the Roan horse, disagreements between Mr. Mechem and Mr. Johnson over treatment of slaves, and the possible connection with Speaker Robinson and his brother-in-law Edmund Chiswell. "The troubling thing about all of this is motive," said Luck. "Why would any of the possible suspects want to murder James Johnson?"

"Murder is rare in Virginia," said Wythe, "especially in this circle of people. It is my experience that when murder occurs, the reasons have to do with money, jealousy, or honor. If money, it is generally in the family and that seems not the case here, unless there is some question of embezzlement of funds by the overseer—perhaps Mr. Johnson had uncovered something that would lead to the firing of Mechem. If jealousy, we probably would have had some rumors of Johnson's infidelity and that seems not the case. If honor, the usual recourse is a dual of some type, legal or not, rather than cold-blooded murder."

"Could Mr. Johnson have known something, potentially damaging to a distinguished person, financial, personal or otherwise?" asked Luck. "That might provide a motive for silencing Johnson."

Wythe thought about Key's remarks. "It is a possibility. If so, it may be difficult to find out the embarrassing information. If it is a secret, those who know the secret will want it to remain hidden. I will sound out some of my colleagues on the matter and see if there are any rumors indicating that possibility. Perhaps I can uncover some information and provide some insight on this point for you and the Sheriff in the investigation."

Wythe indicated that Thomas Jefferson would be over shortly for breakfast. He had suggested that they walk down to the Capitol Building for today's discussion of the Stamp Act. There was a great deal of anticipation about what might occur in the House of Burgesses that day. Much of the speculation centered on Patrick Henry, the relatively new delegate from Louise County, Mr. Key's own home county. Jefferson joined Wythe and Key for breakfast at the Wythe home and then they walked down the Duke of Gloucester Street to the Capitol Building.

Luck was dressed in his finest clothes, which included a long-length linen shirt, breeches, white woolen socks, his new waistcoat that Tom had given him and a jacket. Luck thanked Tom for the waistcoat and Tom replied that it fit Luck perfectly. George Wythe and Thomas Jefferson both looked splendid in their garb. They wore silk waistcoats over their shirts, cravats and doublets—padded jackets with sleeves. Mr. Wythe had on a powdered wig that he only wore for special occasions. Mr. Jefferson wore his long red hair tied behind him. All wore Tricorne hats, which they removed indoors. Key's was a plain black hat, while Wythe's and Jefferson's were edged in gold.

On the way Mr. Wythe gave Luck a short tutorial on the building and roles of the various actors. He explained that the House of Burgesses meets in the Capitol Building, which was originally built in 1704 and rebuilt in 1753 on the same site after a fire had destroyed the original. It is located at one end of the Duke of Gloucester Street— opposite the College of William and Mary, a mile down the street. The Palace Green, in front of Wythe's house, is about half-way from the Capitol Building to the College, so it was a short walk for the three gentlemen.

As they approached the building, Luck noted that it was an unusual H-shaped construction, with two separate two-story brick structures and a large arched passageway between the two, allowing members to be dropped off in bad weather at the brick passageway and to provide access to both sides of the building.

Wythe pointed out that the west structure was the location for the House of Burgesses, which was the "lower house," comparable to Parliament, but with less overall power. "We have certain powers," said Wythe. "For example, all revenue bills are supposed to be introduced in the House of Burgesses, so the enactment of the Stamp Act by Parliament, contrary to the wishes of the House of Burgesses, was a departure from the normal situation and is why the members are so angry at Parliament."

The House of Burgesses was composed of two representatives from each county and individual representatives for the College of William and Mary, and for Jamestown City, Williamsburg, and Norfolk. Wythe noted that he had tried several times unsuccessfully to be elected to the House from his county. Failing that, he had originally been appointed the representative of the College. Now he was elected from his home, Elizabeth City County, where he had his small plantation. They arrived early so that Mr. Key and Mr. Jefferson could take their places in a small gallery near the entrance to the room.

As members of the House of Burgesses arrived, they sat on

either side of the room, with the more senior representatives in the first row and the newer members in the back row. Mr. Wythe took his seat on the left side as he entered the chamber. Other members of the House of Burgesses filtered into the building in a variety of fancy and practical clothing. Mr. Jefferson pointed out some of them to Luck, along with a side comment or two. He noted Carter Braxton was from King William County, as was the murder victim Burgesses James Johnson. John Page was from Gloucester County and a long-time friend of Mr. Jefferson from their studies at the College of William and Mary. Page gave Jefferson a wave as he entered. Richard Henry Lee from Prince William County was regarded as one of the Burgesses' best orators.

"I hope we hear from him today," Jefferson said. Peyton Randolph, the attorney general or Kings Attorney, was a cousin of Jefferson. "A bright legal mind, one of the few attorneys who can occasionally outwit Mr. Wythe," said Jefferson. The two men nodded to one another.

Speaker John Robinson entered looking a bit frail but dignified in his gown and white wig. He was accompanied by his brother-in-law Edmund Chiswell from Middlesex County. "Chiswell has a reputation as a bit of a scoundrel," said Jefferson. "He is quick to anger, and slow to pay off his gambling debts. He trades on the Speaker's name, which bothers me. He is not a person that I enjoy being with, and there are few in this room of whom I would make that statement."

The large room, now about half full, had a curved semicircle at one end, where the House Speaker John Robinson sat in a large eight-foot high carved ceremonial chair, looking very distinguished despite his frailty. Mr. Wythe had told them that the chair was one of the few items saved from the fire that destroyed the original building. In the middle of the room was a table where clerks sat to record the actions of the members. At the end were three large round windows and on each side rectangular windows that together allowed natural light to fill the hall. A candle chandelier in the middle of the room provided additional light as needed.

Mr. Jefferson pointed out to Luck that the power of the British Monarchy was clearly on display. There were larger than life full-length paintings of George II on one side and Queen Caroline on the other. George II, Jefferson noted, was widely admired by Virginians largely because he left them alone. Jefferson said this was very fortuitous, as this long period of "benign neglect" allowed the colonies to develop their own legislatures and structures of governance. "However," said Jefferson, "the presence of the Crown in these portraits is supposed to demonstrate to the House members who really is the controlling political actor."

Luck asked Mr. Jefferson about the rest of the building and the Upper House. Jefferson said that there were three committee rooms upstairs where most of the work of the House took place, bills were referred to and modified or killed by committees. There was also a Committee on Elections where disputed elections were referred to and a joint conference room in the middle of the H shaped building.

On the East side of the Capitol was the Upper House or the Council of Virginia, usually referred to as the Governor's Council. It served a legislative review function, similar to the House of Lords in England, and also a judicial function as the General Court, which was the highest court in Virginia. The twelve councilors were an advisory body to the Governor; they were appointed by the Crown and served as the Governor's cabinet. "They constitute the more conservative large landowners in Virginia," said Mr. Jefferson, "and there are many that believe that there is an inherent conflict of interest as the Council performs legislative, executive, and judicial functions. You can hardly expect them to perform all three roles without some serious problems arising."

As Jefferson was finishing with his comments on the Capitol, all eyes turned to the entrance as Patrick Henry walked in the room. Luck observed that Henry was a tall man, though not as tall as Jefferson, and he had deep set dark eyes that along with his dark hair gave him an air of gravity. Mr. Henry was a newly elected representative from Louisa County and had been sworn in on May 20 as many members were already thinking of heading home. He had won fame as an orator who could capture the attention of any jury and sway them regardless of the law. He had been assisting his father-in-law at Hanover Tavern when he decided to become a lawyer.

"I met Mr. Henry in Hanover when I stayed over at the Tavern on my way to the College of William and Mary. He was a great host and plays a superb fiddle!" said Mr. Jefferson. "He claims he studied only six months before being admitted to the Virginia Bar. I have been studying with George Wythe for three years and am just now feeling competent. He is no legal scholar; although he impressed the examiners with his quick mind. In court he lets his oratory win the argument."

"He won an important case, though, the Parsons Cause," continued Mr. Jefferson to Luck, "and he quickly gained a following in Western Virginia defending the liberties of the common people. When he lacked the argument, he attacked the opposite party, often winning the day. It is what led to his election I am told." Luck sensed a bit of envy in Jefferson's remarks but said nothing. He also had heard about the victories that Henry had secured for the common people with his prevailing oratory. Henry was dressed appropriately in a black outfit with a long red gown, but his wig looked a bit moth eaten and had certainly seen better days.

Everyone in the room now knew that Virginia's agent in London, Edward Montague, who was charged with indicating Virginia's disapproval of the Stamp Act, had sent word that the Stamp Act had been adopted by Parliament—a letter to the House of Burgesses had just arrived by ship. And the Governor also had officially notified them to that effect last week. There was intense anticipation over how the Burgesses would react.

Patrick Henry rose and was recognized by Speaker Robinson. "Mr. Speaker," Henry intoned, "I rise to present a series of resolves against the blatant disregard of the wishes and prerogative of Virginia. There can be no doubt that Parliament no longer regards the colonies as partners or as an essential part of Great Britain. Instead, we are viewed as a mere vassals that must pay homage and tribute to the motherland. We cannot, we must not, allow the Parliament to make a mockery of us. We must assert our own rights forcefully and energetically. During the last few days I was fortunate to work on these resolves with several other gentlemen here today and they have asked me to present the resolves to this body."

Tom Jefferson noted that the Virginia Stamp Act Resolves, as they were called, had been drafted by Henry and several members the previous evening in the Apollo Room of the Raleigh Tavern. Tom had been at the tavern and had listened to their discussion without participating.

One by one Henry read out four Virginia Resolves and asked for discussion and a vote:

Resolved, that the first adventurers and settlers of His Majesty's colony and dominion of Virginia brought with them and transmitted to their posterity, and all other His Majesty's subjects since inhabiting in this His Majesty's said colony, all the liberties, privileges, franchises, and immunities that have at any time been held, enjoyed, and possessed by the people of Great Britain.

Resolved, that by two royal charters, granted by King James I the colonists aforesaid are declared entitled to all liberties, privileges, and immunities of denizens and natural subjects to all intents and purposes as if they had been abiding and born within the Realm of England.

Resolved, that the taxation of the people by themselves, or by persons chosen by themselves to represent them, who can only know what taxes the people are able to bear, or the easiest method of raising them, and must themselves be affected by every tax laid on the people, is the only security against a burdensome taxation, and the distinguishing characteristic of

British freedom, without which the ancient constitution cannot exist.

Resolved, that His Majesty's liege people of this his most ancient and loyal colony have without interruption enjoyed the inestimable right of being governed by such laws, respecting their internal policy and taxation, as are derived from their own consent, with the approbation of their sovereign, or his substitute; and that the same has never been forfeited or yielded up, but has been constantly recognized by the kings and people of Great Britain.

"Mr. Speaker," Peyton Randolph rose to offer another set of Resolves. "While I am in sympathy with the content of Mr. Henry's Resolves, I am unhappy with the length, complexity, and the tone of them. We are British subjects and should acknowledge our duty to follow the laws of Parliament, even if we believe those laws are wrong." Randolph then read his Resolves, which Luck thought made similar objections to the Stamp Act but were much watered down from the stronger, more pointed resolves presented by Henry.

"Mr. Speaker," Henry rose again. "May I suggest to the honorable gentleman that if the currently introduced Resolves fail, we should be glad to consider his milder ones; however, I believe I speak for a majority of the members of the House in saying that now is not the time to be modest, now is the time to be bold and assert our rights—rights that others in England take for granted!"

"Mr. Speaker," Edmund Chiswell rose and was recognized. "We have already relayed our views to Parliament from our Committee on Correspondence. And we have hired representatives to present those views to the Parliament. In their wisdom, Parliament has rejected our views. We are subjects of the British Crown and we are talking about pennies in taxes, which will create no great burden on Virginia. It is time we moved on to other business. Mr. Henry's grandstanding can be forgiven as he is a new member to the House of Burgesses and not well acquainted with our processes."

Mr. Speaker, Henry rose again. "Pennies to some are a hardship to others. We are all not as fortunate as Mr. Chiswell in having a large plantation and a brother-in-law to bail him out if necessary."

"You are insulting me and the Speaker," responded Chiswell. "I demand that you take back those last remarks or I will have satisfaction."

"Gentlemen, please!" said the Speaker. "We will have no personal arguments in the chamber. Let us speak to the issues themselves." Several members yelled "here, here," noting their approval of the Speaker's comments.

Now more members rose to speak. Some favored Henry's Resolves, others the milder resolves of Peyton Randolph. However, it became apparent that the majority favored Henry's position. After a number of comments on both sides of the issue, Richard Henry Lee rose and on being recognized indicated that he had been contemplating some concluding thoughts: "It is true, as some have said, that we have made our case and it was rejected. But was it rejected after careful deliberation? No! Our representatives have told us the Stamp Act was adopted in Parliament without any consideration of the positions we laid out before them, so carefully and judiciously drafted by George Wythe and other members of the Committee on Correspondence. Do we just ignore this outrage of democratic principles?" Some members yelled "No!" in response.

Lee continued, "Some have said that we are talking about mere pennies and ask whether we risk angering the Governor and Parliament over so little? It is not the amount that is important, even though those pennies will make so many things more expensive in Virginia. To many in our commonwealth, already beset by weak prices for tobacco, pennies will cause them additional hardship." Again, cries of "hear, hear."

"What is most important in this debate is the principle and precedence that it is setting. We say we are proud to be part of the British Crown and perhaps we are, but we are not a very important part. We are not an integral part of the body politic in England, merely an appendage that Parliament pays little attention to as long as tobacco and other commodities flow from Virginia to the motherland. Do we have real representation in Parliament?" Lee asked rhetorically. More shouts of "No!"

"Appendages do not need representation Parliament says, they can rest knowing that the body politic will provide them 'virtual representation." Is this what we want? Is this what our loyalty deserve? The answer to both of these questions is a resounding NO! So as much as I am reluctant to poke the hornets' nest over 'pennies,' it is clearly time to make our position clear. We protest and will not support any actions of Parliament for direct taxation on Virginia, without our approval or our representation in Parliament. I thank the gentlemen for their attention." Lee sat down to standing ovation and positive acclaim from the members.

Finally, Henry rose and asked that the question be called on his Resolves—that if voted down, they should consider Randolph's Resolves. Speaker Robinson asked for a vote on Henry's Resolves.

Luck and Thomas Jefferson watched anxiously as votes were taken on each of the resolves. They noted with pleasure that each of the resolves were approved, with a substantial majority, although the more conservative plantation owners in Eastern Virginia tended to be opposed, and the remainder of the representatives from the South and Central Virginia tended to support the Resolves. Some rose to explain their vote and noted that they were conflicted about the Resolves and where things were headed. George Wythe voted in favor of each of the Resolves, though with some trepidation as he felt they were essentially repeating what had originally been sent to Parliament the previous year.

Some members had not expected this new business and had already headed home, so there was not a full House for the votes, which now carried such significance for Virginia and its relationship with Parliament. Increasingly the members sensed a growing tension in the room between the more conservative plantation owners and other representatives who were more inclined to assert the rights of the House of Burgesses.

Patrick Henry stood again and asked leave of the Speaker to present one more Resolve.

"Mr. Henry," said Speaker Robinson, "you have nearly worn us out with your Resolves. What more can be said?"

"The final resolve goes to the heart of our ability to govern ourselves," said Mr. Henry.

Resolved, therefor that the General Assembly of this Colony have the only and exclusive Right and Power to lay Taxes and Impositions upon the inhabitants of this Colony and that every Attempt to vest such Power in any person or persons whatsoever other than the General Assembly aforesaid has a manifest Tendency to destroy British as well as American Freedom.

"You go too far," exclaimed Burgesses and King's Attorney Peyton Randolph. "We are British. There is no such legal entity as America. Our rights and privileges derive directly from the King and Parliament."

"I do not go too far," countered Mr. Henry. "If Parliament and the King will not reconsider, we will have to take other action. Caesar had his Brutus, Charles I his Cromwell, and George III…"

"Treason," yelled Mr. Randolph and Speaker Robinson as many others joined the chorus of yells of opposition.

"and George III may profit by their example. If this be treason, make the most of it." thundered Mr. Henry. More cries of treason and "no" echoed in the chamber.

"Mr. Speaker," George Wythe rose to speak. "Perhaps a little reflection before we accuse someone of treason. I am sure our gentleman from Louisa County was not proposing to overthrow the King, but merely stating with clarity that oppressive measures sometimes lead to unanticipated consequences. Since Parliament chose to ignore our previously agreed to

Remonstrances, it seems that we must assert our own rights in the strongest manner possible. However, while I think this final Resolve is in most respects fitting, I find I must oppose it at this time. Less than half of the members are present. Are we willing to take such strong actions—that go beyond anything we have agreed to previously—without a strong majority vote? I am very troubled by that.”

"The gentlemen is correct that I meant no disrespect to the Crown," said Mr. Henry. "What matters here is our rights as British subjects. In no way would I propose or sanction any action against the King, whom we all admire and who is our Sovereign, but we are protesting the actions of a Parliament that is unaccountable for its actions."

Strong arguments were made on both sides with many members indicating they were uncomfortable with the vote given the absence of so many of the members of the House of Burgesses. The vote on the final resolution was close. The fifth resolve passed by a single vote. Luck heard Peyton Randolph whisper to his cousin Thomas Jefferson that "By God, I would have given 500 guineas for a single vote."

After the vote, the Speaker declared that as there was no other business before the House of Burgesses they were adjourned. The debate and votes had left all of the members strained and drained of all energy. However, as Mr. Henry was leaving, Edmund Chiswell took a few parting shots at the 'upstart,' to some of his friends, but easily overheard by the assembly. Friends of Mr. Henry restrained him from commenting further, though Henry seemed more than willing to take on Chiswell.

❋ ❋ ❋

Luck and Mr. Jefferson joined Mr. Wythe as they walked back to his house for a late dinner. At dinner, all of the talk was about Patrick Henry, Edmund Chiswell and the Resolves and what it is likely to mean for the future of Virginia and its relationship with England.

"I am afraid," said Wythe, "that we are on a collision course with Parliament and it may lead to the eventual dissolution of our current bond with Great Britain."

"Surely not," countered Jefferson. "Will not Parliament reconsider its actions? I am told we have friends in Parliament that will certainly carry our message. Would we risk all to break ties with Great Britain? And would they even let us do so? I can't imagine that they would let us go without a fight, and what chance would we have against the might and power of the British Empire?"

"Sometimes momentum is so strong that good-willed people on both sides of an issue cannot prevent a breech," Wythe noted. "I would not want us to risk a military conflict with Great Britain. How could we possibly win that? And yet I do not see a clear path for compromise with the current government in England."

Luck remained largely silent during the discussions. He did not have the political background or knowledge of his companions and was pleased just to listen to their views and arguments. While both men preached compromise, it seemed to Luck that George Wythe was the more uncertain about likely future events. Thomas Jefferson was more optimistic that a path toward reconciliation was possible, though he too was incensed at the actions of Parliament.

"Do we not have certain inalienable rights," asked Jefferson "to live in peace, to govern ourselves, to work for our own prosperity and the prosperity of the colony? Can Parliament, the King, or anybody take those away from us?"

"As to our rights," said Wythe, "we have had only those granted to us by the Crown. I think that is wrong, but there are many of our fellow planters that feel this has always worked for us and are unwilling to think of other alternatives."

Luck summoned up the courage to ask Mr. Wythe why he had voted against the final Resolve, even though in general agreement with the sentiment. "It was a close decision for me," said Mr. Wythe. "While I was sympathetic with the aim, I was concerned with the timing. More than one-half of our members were not there. It seemed to me that we need to be sure that a strong majority of the members of the House of Burgesses agree with this position before we commit it to history. And I felt it was important for me to not strongly oppose the Speaker at this point. We may need to drive a consensus later on Virginia's position, and I want to be in a position where I can play a role in determining that consensus. But it may be a moot point now. The news of these five Resolves will surely be the talk of Virginia as soon as they are printed in the press."

They talked late into night before breaking up and heading to bed, Luck to his upstairs abode and Thomas Jefferson to his hired rooms in town.

CHAPTER 19

Tuesday May 28

Luck saw George Wythe early Tuesday morning at breakfast: "What did you think of the debate yesterday in the
House of Burgesses?" Key asked Wythe. "I was struck by
the reasoned arguments and the passions of those involved, on
both sides of the issue."

"It made me proud to be a Virginian," said Wythe. "We have
a solid history of self-government. We have fought with the
British against the French and the Indians. We have shown our
abilities. I don't want Virginia to be treated as a child which
must follow its British parent's demands. We are no longer
so dependent on Great Britain. But when Patrick Henry talks
about America, I don't know what that is. We are all individual
colonies and not united in any common undertaking—at least
not at the present."

Luck left to try to meet with the silversmith about the Roan
horse that he saw earlier at the stables behind the Goal. Wythe
went into his study and considered both the murder investigation and the current political situation. Yes, they had passed
Patrick Henry's Resolves, but Wythe had found out that the
Council had surreptitiously deleted the fifth, and most explosive one, from those that went on to the Governor. Even though
he had voted against the fifth resolve, he felt that the unilateral
action by the Council to delete it from the record was devious
and infuriating. On the other hand, the Resolves, including the

fifth one, already were published in the newspaper so the general public, as well as the other colonies, would be aware of the position of the Virginia House of Burgesses.

He was pleased with the result, even if he felt that Virginia politically was hurtling out of control to some future state that he could not yet imagine. He believed it was possible that the thirteen colonies could work together in some form of confederation, but there are so many differences among us, he thought. The South was primarily agricultural and unfortunately relied on slaves for its primary workforce. The North's economy was primarily based on manufacture and those states were largely opposed to slavery. What they shared was a sense of destiny, perhaps, and their general dislike for the oppressive actions of Parliament.

"Who are we anyway?" mused Wythe. "Are we British, Virginians or Americans?" The latter, thought Wythe, seemed to imply that there was something uniting the colonies that to this point had not really materialized. "How would we feel about breaking from our British roots, the monarchy and the notion of ourselves as part of a large empire?" These were likely to be the central questions facing the colonies in the next few years.
Among Wythe's books were those authors who promoted the notions of democracy or consent of the governed, like Locke, and those, like Hobbes, who thought democracy incompatible with the self-interests of mankind. Wythe certainly believed in the notion of self-government and felt that Virginia, as well as most of the colonies, had performed in a satisfactory way in governing themselves. There remained wide-ranging questions about what kind of democracy the colonies wanted and exactly how it would work in practice.

Virginia was primarily ruled by white men of wealth. Yes, they had a form of democratic representation, albeit limited to men of property, somewhat similar to the Senate in ancient Rome. There were advantages to this arrangement, thought Wythe, but in no way could it be considered a full democracy in which most people had votes. Wythe felt that voting should at least extend to all free men.

Wythe generally agreed with John Locke that though we are driven by self-interest, we also are capable of using reason to avoid tyranny. The basis of legitimate government, Locke thought, is authority gained through consent of the governed. The duty of any government is to protect the natural rights of the people, including life, liberty and property. If we have a chance to form our own government, that should be our goal, thought Wythe. But he worried about how the issue of slavery would affect any negotiations about a new government. "We should push for the gradual elimination of slavery in all of the colonies," Wythe thought, though he was unsure whether enough of the states would agree to that idea.

❉ ❉ ❉

As Wythe was contemplating the future of Virginia, Luck was off to see the silversmith James Craig. He had little knowledge of the silversmith's profession, but was interested in it, and he needed to talk to Craig about his Roan horse. Craig was regarded as one of Williamsburg's most accomplished silversmiths and produced a wide range of jewelry, cups, teapots and spoons.

Luck went into the shop and asked for Mr. Craig. There were only two persons in the shop, likely Craig and an apprentice. Luck explained that he was a deputy to Sheriff Norvell. Craig was busy working on a silver ring and he asked Luck to wait until he was finished. At Luck's request, Mr. Craig explained the process.

"We start with a silver rod and file it down until it fits into our draw-plate, which we use to size the width of the ring. Then, estimating the circumference we cut it to the desired length. Using heat, a hammer and mold, we gradually turn it into a circle."

"As you see," continued Mr. Craig, "I have just soldered the ends together to make the ring tight. Finally, a last check on the circumference, to make sure our lady or gentleman will have no trouble putting on the ring. Sometimes we have to heat it up again to adjust for sizing, though not this time—it looks right to me. Finally is the polishing, which I will have my apprentice do while I talk to you. You indicated you are the deputy to Sheriff Norvell; how can I help you?"

"At the Sheriff's request, I am following up on issues related to the investigation of the murder of James Johnson," said Key. "Can you tell me whether you knew James Johnson and had any business with him?"

"Yes, I knew Mr. Johnson, I expect most of the Williamsburg shop owners knew him" said Mr. Craig. "He occasionally bought items here. His daughter is soon to turn sixteen I believe, and he asked me to make a special ring for the occasion. I have a unique 'forever love' item of my own design, which are intertwining silver rings. In fact he picked them up about two weeks ago. He also had a small rosebud engraved on each of the rings."

"Was there any problem with payment? We have been told that Mr. Johnson was in some financial difficulty," asked Luck.

"Well he did pay me," said Mr. Craig. "Of course I would have extended him credit if asked. It was not an extremely expensive gift. Although as I recall, he did come to the shop last year to sell some of his silver items to me, which we melted down for other jewelry and goods. He received the going rate for silver. At the time I did not think anything of it. People often feel that they have extras of some silver items that are not used, so why not sell them for ready cash?"

"In general though," continued Mr. Craig, "silver items are a good way to store your assets. They generally have a use, but can always be turned into cash when necessary."

"Very interesting," said Luck, "I understand that you own a Roan horse."

"Yes, he is a beauty," said Mr. Craig. "I keep him in a stable behind the Public Goal. Why is that of interest?"

"A dark Roan horse was seen tied up in the vicinity of the

Powder Magazine on the night of the murder," answered Luck, "so we are checking with anyone who has a Roan horse. Would you mind telling me where you were last Sunday night?"

"I was not at the Powder Magazine murdering James Johnson," said Craig heatedly. "I am sure I was home all night. So I guess I have an alibi of sorts, although the only people who could vouch for me are my wife, one apprentice, and our one servant who lives with us. You are certainly welcome to talk to them."

"I certainly did not mean to imply that you were responsible," said Key quickly. "But we are hoping that we might find a witness who saw someone or something that might be helpful to our investigation."

Somewhat mollified, Craig calmed down and said, "I wish I could help you. I liked James Johnson and murder is a terrible thing, especially when one has a young wife and daughter. I just don't have any ideas that might be helpful. I cannot imagine the motive and I was not in the proximity of the Powder Magazine on the night of the murder."

Luck thanked Mr. Craig for his time and for the lesson on how silversmiths fashioned items. "I am very impressed with the quality of your work," said Key. "Perhaps one day I will be able to afford to buy a gift from your shop." Craig said he was always welcome and they bade each other good day.

Mr. Wythe had asked the Sheriff if he could borrow back Mr. Key on Tuesday afternoon. He had some correspondence and other work that needed completing and thought he could use Luck's assistance. The Sheriff readily agreed and so after the visit at the silversmiths. Luck headed back to the Wythe house.

The afternoon was filled with a variety of clerical tasks as Luck familiarized himself with the kind of work he would be doing for Mr. Wythe. The work did not have the same level of excitement as when Luck was working for the Sheriff, but he enjoyed listening to Wythe think about issues, legal, political and even personal. He seemed willing to treat Luck as a colleague, rather than just a clerk. Yes the work was somewhat routine, mostly making copies of letters or documents, but there was a logic to it and Mr. Wythe always explained why he was doing something and how important Luck's involvement was to the final outcome.

After an early supper with the family, Mr. Wythe retired to his library for his evening reading, which he tried to do every day. Sometimes Elizabeth would just sit with him, either reading or engaging in one of her crafts. George enjoyed her presence and thought how fortunate he was to have found Elizabeth after the death of his first wife. He loved her very much and the mutual love and affection was evident in all of the little things they did for each other.

Luck had finished Shakespeare's Henry V and thought he would try to read John Locke, as both Mr. Wythe and Thomas Jefferson had quoted him during their discussions Monday evening after the debate over the Stamp Act Resolves. He found the reading a bit difficult but took down a few notes and hoped that he might eventually have time to discuss them with Mr. Wythe or Tom Jefferson.

CHAPTER 20

Wednesday May 29

George Wythe had asked Sheriff Norvell to meet him and Mr. Key over breakfast at the Wythe house. He had planned a nice breakfast and a relaxing atmosphere so that they could discuss the case and plan strategy. Sheriff Norvell arrived promptly at eight as requested and was invited by Wythe to take food at the buffet that had been set up and then come over to the table with him and Luck.

Mr. Wythe's wife Elizabeth was just finishing her breakfast. Norvell thought she was a striking woman and needed no excessive adornments to look every bit the wealthy and confident lady that she was. She greeted the Sheriff and took her leave of the men, indicating that she had other work to do.

The buffet was a rich array of cold and hot items: boiled eggs in egg-shaped ceramic containers; slices of ham that had been smoked and cured in spices, fruit that came from Wythe's garden, bread, butter and marmalade. After helping himself, Sheriff Norvell took his plate to the table.

"Would you prefer coffee, tea, or ale?" asked Mr. Wythe. Sheriff Norvell opted for coffee. He knew that some men preferred ale in the morning, but he liked the taste of coffee and it gave him a jump start to the day.

They enjoyed the breakfast and engaged in light banter about the day, which was unfortunately rainy, the actions of the

House of Burgesses, their Sunday dinner at the Johnson's plantation and a variety of peripheral issues. Luck enjoyed hearing the two men engage in these issues. They both were men of experience, but had different backgrounds and perspectives. Luck thought William Norvell was the more pragmatic of the two. He had several years of experience as Sheriff of Williamsburg and James City County and had dealt with men of high standing as well as those on the marginal end of Virginia society. Thus, he was a bit more cynical in his outlook on events and seemed to favor order over sweeping ideas or generalities.

George Wythe, on the other hand, thought Luck, had a brilliant mind and access, from his library, to all of the current world-views on government. But as an attorney, he had a very analytical mind. Thus, he liked to entertain new concepts, but was careful that they were presented in a measured and thoughtful manner. He sometimes liked to toss out ideas, just to see how others would react. Wythe had told him that Socrates enjoyed this form of learning in his dialogues with colleagues.

"I'd like to present a proposition to you about the murder," said Mr. Wythe, interrupting Luck's thoughts. "Mr. Key mentioned something the other night about the possibility of blackmail as the ingredient that fueled the murder, although he did not use that specific term. I have been thinking of that idea. I don't mean old-fashioned blackmail—cash for secrecy, but we know that James Johnson was in financial difficulty. Suppose he had found out something that concerned one of the leading plantation owners and its disclosure would create fiscal problems for the owner and perhaps destroy his reputation. Mr. Johnson might have felt that this individual was in a position to help him—to loan him money—in return for Johnson's silence."

"That is an interesting idea," said Sheriff Norvell, "but it depends upon several assumptions." The Sheriff thought a few moments before proceeding. "First, there has to be some looming and significant financial or personal scandal among the plantation owners. Second, the knowledge of that scandal would have to potentially ruin the individual, both financially and in terms of his reputation. Third, though apparently a secret, Johnson had to have knowledge of this scandal. And finally, someone decided to kill Johnson to cover it up and protect his, or possibly his family's, wealth and reputation."

"True," said Mr. Wythe. "The proposition does rest upon those assumptions—and they are significant; but what other theories do we have to go on about the murder? Only that James Johnson's former slave Jacob might have had a grudge that could have led him to murder Mr. Johnson, assuming that he could have lured Johnson to the Powder Magazine at midnight! And that seems even more far-fetched to me. Or I guess the possibility that Mr. Mechem decided to ride to Williamsburg from the Johnson Plantation and somehow persuaded Mr. Johnson to meet him at the Powder Magazine—also rather far-fetched."

"Yes, you are correct, but I can't say that I have run across any looming financial problems of the type of magnitude to create a major scandal in my role as Sheriff and tax-collector," said Sheriff Norvell. "No one owes large amounts of taxes that would be cause of scandal. We all have been late paying a time or two and there is no real issue there."

"The one that seems a possibility to me is whether there has been something wrong with the accounting or spending of funds from the Colonial Treasury," said Mr. Wythe. "I know there is a Committee of the House of Burgesses that is examining this issue. I am not on the Committee, but I think that is worth following up on, though of course it is very sensitive. I do not want to cast any dispersion on our Speaker John Robinson and it is hard to see him murdering anyone at his age and relative infirmary."

"An interesting idea," said Sheriff Norvell. "I think it would be worth further investigation and you might be in a position to help us with this. If I start asking questions, members of the House of Burgesses are likely to get defensive. You might be able to talk to them in an informal way and see if there is any truth to the possibility that you suggested."

"I am happy to assist if I can," said Mr. Wythe. "What do you want me to do?"

"Would you speak with some of the members of the Committee or others who might have knowledge of fiscal irregularities and see what you can discover?" asked Sheriff Norvell. "If they are reluctant, you can say that I asked you to do this as I thought it more appropriate than if I do so directly. Information will be kept confidential, unless it bears directly on the murder."

"I will do so," responded Mr. Wythe. "Let's meet up later in the day, perhaps early evening? It may take me some time to find the best people to speak with and some of the members of the House of Burgesses have already left town."

* * *

Having agreed to meet about six in the evening, Luck and Sheriff Norvell left to go to speak with Peyton Randolph to see what he knew about the ownership of the Roan horse mentioned by one of his groomsmen. Sheriff Norvell told Luck that Peyton Randolph was one of Williamsburg's and Virginia's most influential persons. He was born in Tazwell Hall in Williamsburg and spent his entire adult life here. His parents were Sir. John Randolph and Susanna Beverly. His father died when he was sixteen. He attended the College of William and Mary and later studied law at the Inns of Court in London, becoming a member of the Virginia Bar in 1743. He was appointed Attorney General that year and has served in the House of Burgesses since 1751.

Mr. Randolph had represented the House of Burgesses in a battle to prevent a fee for the certification of land patents, defying the Governor at the time. He briefly lost his position as Attorney General to George Wythe, but at Wythe's request was reinstated. Even so, the Sheriff told Luck that it was rumored that there was a bit of rivalry between Mr. Randolph and Mr. Wythe. They had been on opposite sides of many legal cases, as both were regarded as among the finest lawyers in Virginia. "I suppose there is a natural rivalry that occurs when you are arguing against one another in court," said Norvell.

The Sheriff also told Luck that Randolph was regarded as one of the leading members of the Virginia establishment and as such he entertained frequently. It was about that entertainment, particularly the dinner that was attended by the Speaker John Robinson that interested them. They found Randolph at home as they expected. His butler invited them in and, after asking their business with Mr. Randolph, showed them to a parlor where informal meetings were held.

After a short while, Mr. Randolph came down the stairs and into the parlor: "How can I help you gentlemen?" Sheriff Norvell introduced his deputy Luck Key and said, "We are following up on a possible lead with respect to the murder of James Johnson. We have a witness who saw a dark Roan horse tied up near the Powder Magazine the night that James Johnson was killed. We are hoping the individual may have witnessed something that could help us in our inquiries."

"Last Saturday, I spoke to your groomsman James," said Mr. Key, "and he believed that about a month ago he took care of such a horse. He thinks it may have been when you entertained Speaker Robinson and some of his family."

"Well, I can't tell you whether any of the guests owned a Roan horse," answered Randolph, "but late last month I did entertain Speaker Robinson and some of his family, including his daughter, sister and brother-in-law Edmund Chiswell. You will have to speak directly to them about who might be the owner of a Roan horse. But I doubt if any of them would know anything about the murder. Surely they would have come forward if they knew anything."

Sheriff Norvell and Luck looked at one another and remembered that Mr. Chiswell had also been a patron of Chowning's Tavern on the night of the murder. As Sheriff Norvell thanked Mr. Randolph for his information, Randolph asked Mr. Key a question.

"I saw you at the debates on Friday next to Thomas Jefferson, I believe. You and Tom are part of the next generation of Virginians. What did you think of the Resolves that we adopted, without my approval as you might have noted, and Patrick Henry's audacious claims against the Crown?"

Luck thought carefully before responding, knowing that Mr. Randolph had introduced competing, and more moderate, Resolves. "I am from Louisa County and so I am naturally drawn to our representative Patrick Henry. Despite his strong speech, I don't believe he was actually proposing actions against the Crown, but was trying to assert our rights against Parliament. He is a bit rough around the edges, but does seem to have the support of the people of Louisa County."

"I know you had similar Resolves prepared, although not as strident. So I think we all would agree on the aim, to secure some independence from the arbitrary will of Parliament. It is really a question of tactics and, I suppose, tact," Luck concluded. "The question is where we go from here and I am afraid that is beyond my foresight. I am just hopeful that you and other members of the House of Burgesses will find the right path."

"Very diplomatically considered," said Mr. Randolph. "I think Mr. Key has a future in politics Norvell! What do you think Sheriff?"

"Could be," said Sheriff Norvell, as they took their leave. Outside, Norvell turned to Luck and said, "That was a neat trap you managed to escape from. Of course in our positions we are not supposed to be political, but it is hard not to take sides on these issues." They went their separate ways and agreed to meet later at the Wythe house.

CHAPTER 21

George Wythe thought that he should return to Burgesses Carter Braxton and Richard Henry Lee as they promised the best hope of uncovering a potential scandal involving the Treasury, if there was one. He couldn't believe that Speaker Robinson was involved in any financial misdealing, but there had been rumors of problems in the Treasurer's account and the Speaker was also Virginia's Treasurer. When the two positions were merged, it was done because the members of the House of Burgesses felt that the Speaker was not adequately paid for his job, while the Treasurer was entitled to retain 2.5 percent on certain monies raised in the colonies. However combining the positions created possible conflicts of interest thought Wythe and wondered if he should address that issue next year in the House of Burgesses. He agreed with Robert Carter that it was probably right to split the two positions.

Wythe found Carter Braxton at the Raleigh Tavern on Duke of Gloucester Street, an L-shaped, white wooden structure. The tavern, named for Sir Walter Raleigh, was one of the largest in Williamsburg and often the site of impromptu meetings of various factions of the House of Burgesses or for committee work. The Committee on Correspondence had met there last year to frame their objections to the proposed Stamp Act. The Committee met in the large banquet room known as the Apollo

Room and Wythe had been instrumental in the drafting of the message to Parliament, though it apparently had little effect in London.

Built in 1735, the tavern changed owners a number of times but Wythe thought it maintained the spirit of the Latin motto written over the mantel: *Hilaritas sapientiae et bonae vitae proles* translated as "Jollity is the offspring of wisdom and good living." A bust of Sir Walter sat above the entrance door on the portico, encouraging the revelers as they entered, Wythe supposed.

As Braxton had just previously arrived, he invited Wythe to join him for dinner. The Raleigh Tavern was known for its good food and always had freshly made soup that changed daily as well as a Wythe favorite, Peanut Soup, which he ordered along with a Pottage Pye, tender chicken and vegetables in a creamy stew, baked beneath a flaky pastry. He ordered ale and after Braxton had ordered the house soup and the Pottage Pye they started to chat about the recent events.

"Well, that was quite a lot of excitement in the House of Burgesses on Monday," said Braxton. "I noted that you and I were on the same side on some of the Resolves, including the fifth Resolve, which seemed far too extreme to me."

"I can understand why you might feel that way," said Wythe. "A little more diplomatic language would have made the Resolves more palatable to more of the members. I was frankly surprised that the fifth Resolve was adopted, even if by only one vote. I agreed with the sentiments, but felt that since less than half of the members were present, we should not adopt such a wide-ranging statement of independence without a clear majority, so I ended up voting no as you did."

"What I think it shows," Wythe continued, "is the growing sentiment that Parliament is not really concerned with the views of the elected representatives of Virginia or, for that matter, with the issues that concern the people in our colony and in the other colonies as well. I think we are at a tipping point; there is a strong movement for change, but I am not sure its size, or direction, or staying power."

"Interesting observation," said Braxton. "I have always been a loyal follower of the Crown, but am beginning to believe that we may need to strongly assert our prerogatives. Just how we do that, without completely breaking with Great Britain is a difficult question. To change subjects, what have you heard about the investigation into the death of James Johnson?"

Wythe provided Braxton a brief update on where Sheriff Norvell was in his investigation. "The problem continues to be motive. One theory that we have been considering is that the murderer may have been trying to hide a scandal of some kind. James Johnson may have had information on the issue and felt that he could leverage that information to, perhaps, secure a loan or other financial benefit. I am hoping as a close friend of his that you might have some idea about what James was thinking about that may have led to the clandestine meeting and murder."

Braxton thought and took some time to respond. "About two weeks ago, James and I had a discussion concerning rumors about the Treasury. Some of the plantation owners, myself included, have received financial help from Speaker Robinson, who said they were from his own personal funds. I do not know how much the lending might total, whether we are talking about hundreds or thousands of pounds. And Robinson is one of the wealthiest men in Virginia, so perhaps he could afford to personally lend that amount. You may remember that two years ago the House of Burgesses asked three members, Richard Bland, Richard Henry Lee and Benjamin Harrison, to examine the accounts after some Glasgow merchants had raised doubts as to whether some redeemed notes that had supposedly been destroyed, had in fact been destroyed. If they were not, then there could be additional funds floating in Virginia that would, at least in the short-term, provide relief to some of the planta-tion owners in trouble."

Wythe said he did remember and recalled that at the time the three member committee had not found anything wrong. "But my impression was that it was a very cursory investigation. Hasn't a new investigation been instituted by the Burgesses?"

"Yes," said Braxton. "In addition to the original three members, four more were added, John Page, Dudley Diggs, Archibald Cary and Lewis Burwell; but they have not yet reported their conclusions. I suppose it is possible that Johnson found out about some of their expected findings and hoped to leverage that information into receiving a loan from Speaker Robinson. John Page was close to James Johnson and might have given him the impression that there was something wrong with the Treasury accounts. But of course you don't believe that Robinson would have killed Johnson to keep that secret."

"No, that hardly seems likely," said Wythe, "especially given the Speaker's age and general health. But could someone else have tried to cover it up? Someone who faced substantial loses if the Treasury issue was revealed and led to financial problems for Speaker Robinson?"

"I am not sure who that would be." Braxton. "I suppose potential heirs might be concerned about their inheritance. Though is that a strong enough motive for murder?"

"Money and honor, two powerful motives," speculated Wythe. He took his leave at that point and thought he would try to speak with Richard Henry Lee or any other member of the House of Burgesses serving on the special committee that was still in Williamsburg.

Fortunately, he was able to track down Mr. Lee at the Capitol Building. He had spoken to Lee once and thought perhaps given the stage of the investigation, Mr. Lee might be more forthcoming on the report of the newly formed special committee to examine the Treasury. Lee was finishing up some other committee business. When Wythe indicated that he wanted to talk about the special committee, Lee suggested that they take a walk outside, so they would not be overheard.

"As you know," said Lee, "we are trying to see whether the books balance and whether there were any indiscretions in actions by the Speaker, as Treasurer. It has been hard to get everyone on the committee together—all seven of us—and that has resulted in some delay. I think most of the committee seem prepared to again say that nothing is wrong. We have given the Treasurer wide discretion over how Treasury funds are used or invested when not needed."

"However," continued Lee, "it looks to me like the Speaker was not as careful as he should have been about which funds were Treasury funds versus his personal funds. There seems some intermingling that I can't sort out. Also, there is no record of the British notes used to fund the recent war with the French and Indians. Those notes were redeemed and presumably destroyed by the Treasurer, but I have been unable to find any record of such destruction. That is what the Glasgow merchants were concerned about a couple of years ago, when this issue was first raised."

"Would James Johnson have been aware of the potential problem for Speaker Robinson?" asked Wythe.

"It is possible." said Lee. "Although James was not on the special committee, he was close friends with John Page, who *is* on the special committee. They often stayed in the same lodgings during the House of Burgesses sessions. It would not surprise me if Page made some comments about his own thinking, which to some extent parallels my own on the matter. Frankly, even if the rumors are true and the Speaker was using Treasury funds to loan to other plantation owners, I would not be surprised if the current committee again finds nothing wrong—as some of them, myself included, have been beneficiaries of the Speaker's actions. So we are likely to see another report that finds no wrongdoing."

❋ ❋ ❋

Wythe, Norvell and Key reconvened at six that evening to compare notes and decide what to do going forward. Sheriff Norvell thought that the information from Wythe did make a case that James Johnson may have found out about the problems in the Treasury, perhaps from John Page, perhaps others. Whatever his information, Johnson might have felt that he could leverage that information into gaining financial support from Speaker Robinson. "We all agree that the Speaker is an unlikely murderer—his age and health seems to preclude that possibility," said Johnson.

"Among the possible heirs to the Speaker Robinson's estate," asked Wythe, "who has the most to lose if this information becomes public?"

Luck noted that Edmund Chiswell, Robinson's brother-in-law, had dined at Chowning's the night of the murder; that he may be the owner of the Roan horse that Jacob claims to have seen that night near the Powder Magazine; and that a scandal would likely affect him both personally and financially. Wythe said that Thomas Jefferson had felt that Chiswell was a bit of a scoundrel, and we saw in the House of Burgesses that he has quite a temper.

"I think our next step is to interview Chiswell," said Sheriff Norvell. "But even if Mr. Key's speculation is accurate. What do we have as real proof? We have proximity, Chowning's Tavern and the Roan horse. But the horse sighting and the timing of that sighting is only by one person—Jacob, a slave. Will a jury likely believe Jacob or Edmund Chiswell? I would not want to rest this case on the slim likelihood that they will believe Jacob. Further, we don't know the financial relationship that might exist between Speaker Robertson and his brother-in-law Mr. Chiswell. Absent a confession, what is our real proof that Chiswell is guilty or even has a strong motive?"

"Even if I think Edmund Chiswell is guilty," continued the Sheriff, "I don't see how I could arrest him on the flimsy proof we have to date. And can you imagine the political ramifications of making such a charge against the Speaker's brother-in-law?"

"You have to do what you think is right," said Wythe. "For what it is worth, I will back your decision completely and try to provide whatever political cover that you might need. But I do understand your dilemma; we just don't seem to have enough facts to make a case."

Norvell and Key agreed to meet at seven the next morning to ride out to Edmund Chiswell's plantation and speak with him

❋ ❋ ❋

That evening Luck came into the Wythe library and asked if he could bother Mr. Wythe with a question that had come up. Wythe said, "of course, what is on your mind."

"This is not really directly related to the investigation, at least I don't think so. When I went next door to Mr. Robert Carter's house I spoke with two Negro gentlemen who were servants of Mr. Carter, but they told me that Carter had freed them. It made me think of my own attitude about slavery. Is it right for a person to own another human being? I can understand the concept of an indentured servant. My great-grandfather paid to bring over from England some individuals who otherwise would not have been able to afford the trip. In return, they agreed to work for him for a period of years—seven I believe— and then they would be free to continue working for him for wages or find other employment."

"But slavery is different," continued Luck. "It is not a voluntary arrangement. Jacob was stolen from his parents when he was just a boy and brought over to Virginia. He is fortunate that the blacksmith may eventually provide him freedom, but what of all of the other slaves who have no hope to enjoying what we take for granted? And what about the owners of slaves who are brutal or otherwise take advantage of them?"

"Robert Carter, as well as many individuals in Virginia have condemned slavery, but they are in a minority," said Wythe. "And the majority feel that slave labor is the only way the tobacco economy in Virginia can continue. I am not sure of that view, and I have been a strong advocate for eliminating the im-

155

portation of slaves and of finding a way to gradually free them, or provide them legal manumission, as it is referred to."

Wythe walked over to the library and picked up a small pamphlet. "My great-grandfather, George Keith, was active among the Quaker community and as early as 1690 was condemning the slave trade. He noted that port scenes provided a disgusting evidence of the evils: stinking slave boats, sick and miserable human cargo, demeaning slave auctions, where Negroes, young or old, male or female, were stripped naked and mauled by potential buyers. In 1693 he wrote perhaps the first anti-slavery treatise published in America. Primarily aimed at the Quaker community, it was entitled, *Exhortation and Caution to Friends Concerning Buying or Keeping Negroes*."

"He argued in the pamphlet that true Christians could not participate in this inhumane treatment of other people," Wythe continued. "He urged Quakers to only purchase workers with the idea of educating them and giving them their freedom. And he argued that slavery violated five tenets of the scriptures: first, they were dealing in stolen goods in direct conflict with the eighth commandment against stealing; second, the practice violated Christ's admonition to 'do unto others as you would have them do unto you'; third, scriptures state that people should not return runaway slaves but harbor them and teach them the Gospel; fourth, Quaker involvement in slavery debased the mission of Christianity; and finally, earthly riches acquired by exploiting others are corrupt and contemptible."

"It seems to me," said Wythe, "that those tenets also argue for the abolition of slavery completely. There are many admirers of Keith's arguments, including Philadelphia's Benjamin Franklin, and I am persuaded that this is an evil institution in Virginia and throughout the South—there are fewer slaves in the North and a greater sentiment for freeing them."

"Of course, you may feel that I am a hypocrite, as I own slaves, despite my beliefs. I inherited these individuals or they were given to me and my wife upon my marriage to Elizabeth. I don't feel totally free to do as I would wish," said Wythe. "I admire what Richard Carter has done so far and have been planning on a similar undertaking myself. Still, there is no doubt that I along with most of Virginia's middle and upper classes benefit from slave labor. I think about this often and hope that changes will occur in my lifetime."

Luck asked to borrow Keith's pamphlet so he could read it that night and Wythe readily agreed. He thought that this subject would have to be something he spent more time considering before he could fully frame his own thoughts. In the gentrified environment of Williamsburg, most of the slaves served as servants in one way or another. They did not have the backbreaking labor that he had seen slaves endure on plantations. When he was an apprentice to Mr. Byers, he often worked side-by-side with Negro slaves in the tobacco fields. But unlike the slaves, he was never beaten by the overseer. And when he was sick or needed a break, he took time off, without fear of physical punishment for his actions. And Mr. Byers was considered a 'good' master compared to some that he had heard about.

However, thought Luck, whether an overseer or owner was good or mean, accommodating like the blacksmith with Jacob, or punishing as Jacob described the Overseer John Mechem, there remained the basic question. Can one person morally justify owning another person? Luck was beginning to think the answer to that question had to be no. But what does that mean for the economy in Virginia and the South that was built on slave labor. After the Johnson Inquest, Bethany had suggested that "you men will have to figure that out." But was this a solvable problem, Luck wondered.

CHAPTER 22

Thursday May 30

Sheriff Norvell picked Key up at the Wythe house at seven. It would be a long ride out to Edmund Chiswell's plantation. Norvell was dressed as usual, however he wore his sword, which he seldom did and Luck spotted a pistol tucked into Norvell's waistcoat. Key, of course, was unarmed. They expected Mr. Chiswell to be at his plantation, because he had left Williamsburg and indicated to other members of the House of Burgesses that he was fed up with politics in Williamsburg and was heading home.

Chiswell's plantation Honeysuckle was adjacent to that of Speaker John Robinson's Heweck Plantation along the Rappahannock River, near the entrance to the Chesapeake Bay. Heweck Manner was built in 1678 by Christopher Robinson, clerk of Middlesex County, and his grandson John Robinson was born in the house. The plantation itself constituted one of the larger land holdings in Virginia. Speaker Robinson had carved out part of his holdings for his brother-in-law at the time of his marriage to Susanna Chiswell. It was his third marriage.

They mostly rode in silence along a route that parallels the beautiful York River, formed by the confluence of the Mattaponi and Pamunkey Rivers. It is not an especially long river, only 34 miles, but with deep channels providing great navigation to and from the Chesapeake Bay, making it one of the important commercial rivers in Virginia. As an estuary it is a combination of fresh and saltwater, with great fishing opportunities. It was the home of the Powhatan Confederation of Native American Indians, but they had been largely driven out by new settlements. The Sheriff commented that he felt some regret for the colonist actions against the Native Indians, the First People in America.

"It is a moral failing on our part that we were unable to find a way to live in harmony with the Indians. Our world-views are so different, though. We treat the land as ours, to buy, sell, and develop. The Indians treat the land as a collective good. So perhaps there was no possibility of harmony—and frankly little thinking on our part about the consequences to Indians of our actions."

"I have a question for you that may seem a little strange," said Luck, "but relates to this idea of morality or ethics and leadership. Mr. Wythe has encouraged me to read daily from his many library books and I first selected Shakespeare's *Henry V*, and I wondered if you have read the play? If so, I have been thinking about something that happened in the play and wanted to get someone else's perspective on it."

"It's been a number of years ago, but yes," said Norvell, "I have read the play, and like many young British boys had to memorize Henry V's St. Crispin's Day Speech—a memorable speech, whether he said those exact words or not, and it led to a glorious victory for the English against the French on the fields of Agincourt. What specifically is your question about the play?"

"Well my knowledge of Henry V is limited," said Key. "I know that he led a rather wild life as a young Prince and one of his friends was Bardolph, who was part of the entourage of Sir John Falstaff. Bardolph followed Henry over to France and was promoted to the rank of lieutenant. However, Henry had given a strict order against looting the local cities that surrendered and Bardolph was discovered stealing from a church in a conquered French town. The punishment for disobeying an order of the King is hanging and he is sentenced to die. In one sense the ethics are clear: Bardolph disobeyed the King's order, so he must bear the consequences."

"Henry could have intervened on the basis of past friendship and he must have been sorely tempted to do so, but instead he had the sentence carried out. What would you have done in a similar situation?" asked Key. "The sentence seems harsh relative to the crime committed and who would have begrudged Henry had he shown some mercy to his former friend."

"You ask, what I would have done?" said Norvell. "Since I am not a King or Prince, but just a Sheriff, I might have shown mercy to Bardolph and found some lesser punishment that more fit the crime. Perhaps that would have been the ethical response. But remember, Henry was in a foreign land, besieged by forces larger than his own. Discipline was essential. Could Henry pardon Bardolph and then hang someone else who had disobeyed him? No. That would greatly weaken his position with his men—it would show a lack of consistency."

"Perhaps one of the most essential qualities of leadership is integrity," continued Norvell. "That is a somewhat all-encompassing virtue, but among its characteristics, I believe, are the notion of consistency in your actions and being true to you word. If someone you work for is deceitful, or tells you one thing today, and another tomorrow, are you likely to want to follow that person?"

"No, I can see what you mean. But don't all leaders sometimes have to hedge the truth, in return for some greater good? Or is that just a justification for their actions?" asked Key.

"It's true that Kings or other leaders of nations must sometimes bend the truth to achieve their ends, which might be in that nation's interest. But it seems to me," said Norvell, "that those instances are rare. People will more likely follow leaders who are honest with them, who are consistent, who admit when they don't know the right answer and who are willing to correct wrong decisions. To me, this type of integrity provides the deepest level of commitment to the people they serve. Too often lies become a habit and are mainly for the benefit of the liar, not the general good."

"Well, you have certainly gotten off to a good start with your readings," continued Norvell. "I am sure that Mr. Wythe would be delighted that you are considering these type of ethical questions as you read. You will have to ask him some of his views on this topic. But for me, George Wythe represents a leader of integrity, someone I could certainly follow and even more importantly has the respect of his fellow Burgesses and the people in general. Anyway, you gave me a chance to think about the issue of leadership, which is likely to be critical for Virginia in the coming days."

They crossed the York River by ferry and went through West Point towards what was referred to as the Middle Peninsula, which contained many plantations and the important town of Urbanna, named for Queen Ann. They stopped at the Black Horse Tavern at West Point for an early dinner before riding out to the plantation.

They arrived in the early evening at the Chiswell plantation Honeysuckle, so named for the bushes that graced the entry-way to the manor house. They were red and yellow and gave off a strong, sweet smell that was fruity with hints of honey and ripe citrus. Norvell noted that an interesting aspect to the bush is that it gives off one smell during the day and a slightly different one in the evening, heady and nectarous—like jasmine tinged with honey.

There were always birds and bees among the Honeysuckle bushes, providing their own symphony of sound. Norvell said he has some of the bushes at his plantation home, but not nearly so many as here. He wondered if this was a particular favorite of Edmund Chiswell's wife Mary.

They rode up to the manor house and were welcomed by a plantation servant and shown into the parlor. Norvell asked the servant to take care of the horses and he agreed to do so. Master Chiswell was out riding his horse, the servant said, but expected back soon. His wife Mary came downstairs to greet them. "You gentlemen look like you have had a long ride," said

Mary. "I will have some refreshments brought in for you. Was Edmund expecting you?"

"No," said Norvell. "I am Sheriff Norvell and my deputy is Mr. Key. We have come to a certain impasse in our investigation into the death of Burgesses James Johnson. We are hoping that Edmund will be able to assist us. I have talked with him once, but now with additional information we need to talk to him again."

"We loved the bright colors and smell of your Honeysuckle plants as we rode into your plantation," said Key. "They must be a favorite of yours or your husband to have so many plants and to name the plantation after them."

"Oh, they are my favorite," said Mary, "and also were the favorite of my mother. It was my idea to name the plantation for the flowers and Edmund graciously agreed with the idea."

Mary was a nice looking woman, perhaps not the beauty of either Sarah or Bethany Johnson, but she had a relaxed, yet dignified demeanor. She was wearing a simple dress and wool shawl, her hair tied up behind her. Key noticed that she also was wearing a set of intertwined rings on her right hand—similar to the rings the silversmith James Craig had described making for James Johnson, which were still missing.

When Mary excused herself to check on something with the servants, Luck quietly told the Sheriff about the rings. "They could be the rings that James Johnson bought, intending them for his daughter Bethany."

"Can Edmund Chiswell have taken the rings from Johnson?" asked Norvell. "If so, that would have been a reckless act."

Their discussion was interrupted by the sound of a horse riding up to the manor house. Deciding to intercept Edmund Chiswell outside, Norvell and Key went out to meet him. "I am surprised to see you Sheriff Norvell," said Chiswell. "I thought I had given you all of the information that you might need for your investigation when we previously met. And I suppose this is your deputy Luck Key, whom I have heard about."

"Yes, this is my deputy," said Norvell. "We are here because we have additional information and need to ask you a few more questions. That is a beautiful Roan horse. Have you had it long?”

The Roan horse was black with white hairs intermingled, giving the body an almost dark-blueish tint. The horse's face and legs were black. It really was a striking horse thought Key, and very much the type of horse that Jacob had described.

“Yes, I have had this Roan for a long time,” said Mr. Chiswell. “He is my favorite horse and only I ride him. But I am sure you did not come all this way to talk about my horse.”

“Actually,” said Norvell, “your horse is one reason why we are here today. It was seen by a Williamsburg resident hitched to a fence near the Powder Magazine about the time of the murder.”

“Well I do not know who provided that information,” Edmund Chiswell countered, “but I am sure they must have their time wrong. It is true that I tied the horse up near the Magazine, but that was only while I was in Chowning's Tavern. I supposed I arrived at the Tavern about nine in the evening and stayed about two hours—I wasn't really paying particular attention to the time.”

“Why didn't you leave the horse behind Chowning's?” asked Norton. “Isn't that where most guests leave their horse as the tavern advertises grazing for horses behind the tavern? It seems strange to me that you would leave the horse tied up across the street near the Powder Magazine.”

“Nonetheless, that is what I did,” said Chiswell. “I probably wanted a bit of a walk to the tavern and back afterwards. Let us go inside. I am thirsty and we can talk further in the parlor.”

They followed Chiswell back into the parlor and Sheriff Norvell tried to think of what strategy he might use to shake Chiswell's story. As of now, despite the fact that Chiswell admitted to hitching his horse to a fence near the Powder Magazine, they had only Jacob's word as to the time. Chiswell seemed calm and unconcerned about the line of questioning. Mary came in and provided the men some refreshments, some juice, pastries and coffee. “Would you prefer something stronger, ale or whiskey?” asked Mary.

"No thank you," said Norvell. "What you have offered us is very nice of you and a welcome respite after our long ride."

After Mary had left, Sheriff Norvell asked Mr. Chiswell to walk them through his movements on that Sunday night. Chiswell seemed a little bemused by the question but went ahead anyway. "I have lodgings with Mrs. McIntyre on South England Street. It is a convenient location when the House of Burgesses is in session. I will often have dinner or supper with my brother-in-law, John Robinson, but Sunday night I had agreed to have supper with a couple of other Burgesses, John Page and Richard Adams. They wanted to talk over legislative strategy for the session. It was rumored that Patrick Henry had planned to introduce a set of Resolves in opposition to the Stamp Act and we wanted to discuss what our position would be on the matter."

"We didn't really have a consensus. Adams had to leave first, perhaps at half eleven, and I spent another half hour or so with Page, talking about other matters. I am sure that I left Chowning's about eleven, walked to my horse and then rode to my lodgings. Mrs. McIntyre has a small stables in back of her house where I keep my horse."

"Mr. Page is on the special committee looking at the issue of loans to plantation owners from your brother-in-law Speaker Robinson and possible concerns about the use of Treasury funds, I believe," said Norvell. "Did that topic come up for consideration?"

"I don't really remember talking about it," said Chiswell. "And you know that no one has come up with any evidence suggesting wrongdoing by the Speaker."

"Had James Johnson approached you for help in getting a loan from Speaker Robinson?" asked Norvell. "Did you not often act for your brother-in-law on some of these legal and financial issues?"

"No, Mr. Johnson did not approach me for a loan, and yes, I do provide some assistance to my brother-in-law, as he is very busy with business of the House of Burgesses," answered

Chiswell.

"Were you at all concerned that James Johnson might spread rumors about the finances of the Treasury and the Speaker's actions? You would have been concerned about that I imagine," said Norvell.

Edmund Chiswell now grew agitated by Norvell's questioning. "I don't know what you think you know about the operations of the Treasury, but I am confident that the current special committee examining the issue will find that everything is in order—just as the last committee did," said Chiswell. "So there is nothing that Mr. Johnson could have said that would have made any difference. I really don't know what you are trying to prove Sheriff. I would be very careful before making any accusations."

"I always try to be careful," said Norvell. "But it does seem to me, that had James Johnson come to you and demanded a loan from your brother-in-law, in return for keeping silent about what he might know about Treasury operations, you might be concerned for your brother-in-law, and possibly for your own reputation."

"This is all nonsense," said Chiswell as he stood up abruptly indicating that he had finished answering. Chiswell was a tall man and used his size to try to intimidate them, thought Luck. The Sheriff reacted powerfully, quietly reasserting his own authority.

"Well, it may or may not be nonsense," said Norvell, "but I am in charge of the investigation and your relationship with the Speaker will not deter me from examining all possibilities."

Mary came in and asked if Sheriff Norvell and Mr. Key would be staying for supper or needed lodgings for the night. Her husband said, "No, they are not staying and will be leaving shortly."

"That is very kind of you to offer," said Norvell as he and Key stood up. "Those are beautiful, unusual rings you are wearing on your right hand. I have wanted to give something like that to my daughter, as you may know, I am a widower."

"Edmund just gave me the rings last week," said Mary. "It was a surprise gift and I love them."

"Can you tell me where you bought the rings, so I might try to find ones like them?" the Sheriff asked Edmund Chiswell.

"At one of the Williamsburg silversmith shops," said Chiswell arrogantly. "I can't remember which one. And I think it is time for you both to go." He walked out with them while the servants retrieved Norvell's and Key's horses.

"I will check out your story with John Page and Mrs. McIntyre," said Norvell. "And we happen to know that James Johnson bought rings very much like the ones Mary is wearing and he might have had them on him when he was killed. They are very distinctive rings and are each engraved with a small rosebud. While I find it surprising that you might have had something to do with Johnson's death, it looks to me like that is a possibility. You might want to think over your actions and if you have any more to tell me, I would appreciate your coming into Williamsburg."

"Is that an order?" asked Chiswell, clearly irritated and upset by the line of questioning.

"At this point it is a request," said Norvell. "But if your story is not backed up by the facts, you seem to be implicated in James Johnson's death."

Luck could see the sweat pouring from Edmund Chiswell's reddening face.

"I can't believe you are threatening me," said Chiswell. "When others here about this, there may be consequences for you."

"Oh, I don't think so," said Norvell. "It is true that Speaker Robinson is well loved and respected but James Johnson was well liked as well and I don't believe anyone in the House of Burgesses would want to cover up his death, despite the politics."

Luck and the Sheriff left the plantation and decided to stop in Urbanna for supper and lodgings for the night, as it would be too late to return to Williamsburg. Urbanna was one of the primary port where tobacco owners would bring their goods for shipment and sale. The town was founded in the mid-1600s by Ralph Wormeley, who patented 3,200 acres on the Rappahannock River and created his plantation, Rosegill. Because of the good dockage, it became one of the twenty designated port towns in Virginia. Though its population was small, Urbanna boasted a classical courthouse and the James Mills Scottish Factor Store, a large warehouse building that contained the tobacco before shipment overseas.

More importantly, for Norvell and Key, Urbanna had a small but popular tavern on Prince George Street where they could have supper and discuss the next steps in the investigation. Urbanna was a fishing town, in addition to its important role in the tobacco trade, and one of its noted catches was oysters. Luck had never had an oyster before, but at Norvell's urging tried a couple of them, which were baked on the half-shell with some kind of breading and seasoning. It was quite unusual.

After the oysters came chicken, potatoes, bread and ale. Norvell and Key discussed the Chiswell interview. Luck summed up his thoughts. "Edmund Chiswell had been at the scene at the time of the murder, or shortly before. He had been having supper with John Page, a member of the special committee investigating the finances of the Treasury. Mr. Page was a friend of James Johnson and lodged at the same guest house with him when in Williamsburg. Chiswell's Roan horse was seen by Jacob at midnight near the Powder Magazine, or at least that is what Jacob claims. It is possible, though not likely, that he saw the horse earlier than that. We could certainly find out when Jacob left the plantation where his wife and children live," said Key. "From that we could estimate the hour Jacob would have arrived back in Williamsburg."

"True, although we are not going to be able to prove that Jacob was there close to midnight. The most damming evidence may be the silver rings," said Norvell. "Mr. Chiswell had no satisfactory explanation for them, and we can easily check to see if similar rings were sold to him by James Craig or another silversmith. While all of this is circumstantial evidence, it is a significant amount of evidence, certainly enough to bring Chiswell in for further questioning."

"Before going further," thought Norvell out loud, "I wonder whether we should pay another visit to Speaker Robinson. His plantation, Hewick, is just on the other side of town. I think politically, it may make sense for me to alert him to our concerns about his brother-in-law. He should be at his plantation as the House of Burgesses has finished business for the year." They decided to do so first thing the next morning before returning to Williamsburg.

❋ ❋ ❋

While the Sheriff and Luck were interviewing Mr. Chiswell, George Wythe went next door to talk to his neighbor Robert Carter. He waited until after dinner time as he did not want to arrive at a time that Carter might feel would require an invitation. He liked Carter, but felt that coming at dinner time would be an intrusion, even for neighbors.

Daniel answered the door and ushered Mr. Wythe into the parlor, coming back before long and inviting Mr. Wythe to join Mr. Carter in the garden. He was seated on a veranda at the back of the house, enjoying the fine day, and rising said, "George, my friend, please take a seat. I will ask Mr. Daniel to provide us some refreshments. It is always good to see you, whether for business or pleasure."

"Business this time, Robert, although I am always pleased to see you too" said Wythe. "As you know, I am helping Sheriff Norvell a bit with his investigation into the murder of James Johnson. One possible theory is that Johnson had some inside information about a possible scandal—perhaps financial—and that he was killed to prevent the disclosure of that information. Without asking you to betray the confidences of the Governor's Council, could that have been a possible reason?"

Robert Carter considered the question and how much he thought he could reveal. "The Council has for some time been concerned about how Virginia finances are being stated in the ledgers. Since I know that the House of Burgesses has a committee examining the issue, we are letting them take the lead. However, some of us in the Council have been discussing with the Governor the need to split the duties of the Speaker and the Treasurer. You know my views on this matter. There are just too many opportunities for financial self-dealing with this arrangement."

"I am coming to that same conclusion. What can you tell me about the Speaker's brother-in-law Edmund Chiswell," asked Wythe.

Carter grew angry. "He is a braggart and a liar and I do not use those terms loosely. I think he has taken advantage of his position with the Speaker to his own financial gain. And I have seen him take a whip to one of his slaves for simply not being as fast as Chiswell wanted. He is known for his temper and I will not play cards with the man or otherwise socialize with him. I am sorry to be so strong, but he is one of the few people here in Williamsburg during the session that I go out of my way to avoid talking to."

After asking about Robert's large family and he about Elizabeth, they exchanged gossip about the Stamp Act Resolves and Parliament's likely response. "I hope we can reconcile with them," said Carter. "I frankly am worried that hot-heads on both sides will lead us into a military conflict. And I don't see how anyone can win that one."

Wythe agreed, took his leave and headed back to his home.

CHAPTER 23

Friday May 31

After a quick breakfast at the Urbanna Tavern, Norvell and Key rode the short way to Hewick, which was named after the ancestral estate in England of Robinson's first wife. Robinson's mansion was indeed splendid and they both marveled at the acres and acres of planted tobacco, as well as the well cultivated gardens and grounds around the mansion, a large brick L-shaped structure that seemed almost like two houses had been joined together.

"It must take an enormous amount of capital, including slaves, to operate this plantation," said Key. Norvell agreed.

Their approach was noticed by Robinson's servants who met them at the front of the house and took care of their horses. Henry, Robinson's butler, indicated that Robinson was home but not feeling well. He showed them into the parlor and said he would ask Robinson if he was able to meet with the gentlemen. They declined refreshments and waited to hear whether Robinson could see them.

After about a half hour, Robinson came downstairs dressed in a robe and came into the parlor. Without his wig and imposing chair of office, Robinson seemed to Luck somewhat diminished in comparison to the regal person he had just seen on Monday.

"I hope this is important," said Speaker Robinson; "had it been anyone but you William, I would have declined to see you.

I have not been very well and the session of the House of Burgesses was very stressful."

"I am extremely sorry to disturb you," said Norvell. "But it is important and I wanted to see you before taking any further action." Speaker Robinson nodded and Norvell briefly described their visit yesterday with Edmund Chiswell. He left out any speculation on the motive, but focused on the fact that Chiswell's horse was seen near the Powder Magazine the night of the murder and that he had given his wife a set of silver intertwined rings that they believed had probably belonged to James Johnson.

"But assuming this is all true," asked Speaker Robinson, "why would Edmund have killed Johnson? Surely not for the rings. He is wealthy and not a thief. What was the motive here?"

"That is the critical question," said Norvell. "We believe that James Johnson knew or thought he knew some facts about the use of Treasury funds and was trying to leverage that knowledge, to have Edmund intervene on his behalf with you to get a loan. Mr. Johnson's financial situation was getting desperate. Perhaps Edmund met Mr. Johnson at the Powder Magazine and tried to reason with him and failing that struck the fatal blow."

Robinson slumped down in his chair and held his head in his hands. "How can this be? Is it really possible that Edmund would have taken that action, thinking he was saving me embarrassment?"

"Edmund claims that he bought the rings from a silversmith in Williamsburg and that he was at his lodgings before the murder occurred. We can check both of these facts and will do so before taking any further action. But I thought it was important for me to explain the situation to you," Norvell said.

"I do appreciate you telling me of your concerns about Edmund and updating me on the investigation. I would not ask you to do anything other than your job," said Speaker Robinson. "I can't tell you how shocked I am about this news and I hope on further investigation you will come up with evidence that points in some other direction."

Norvell said that he hoped so as well. Declining any refreshments and noting how tired Speaker Robinson looked and acted, Norvell and Key took their leave and after retrieving their horses began the long ride back to Williamsburg. Again they rode mostly in silence, though Luck did ask why they had provided Speaker Robinson with all of the evidence that might point to his brother-in-law Edmund Chiswell.

"I wanted to see his reaction," said Norvell, "and, unless he greatly misled us, he was shocked to hear about Edmund Chiswell's possible involvement. I did not expect that the Speaker would be involved, but that reaction convinced me that if Chiswell did murder James Johnson he did so without the knowledge or approval of Robinson. I expect we will see the Speaker also speaking to his brother-in-law. Perhaps Edmund will turn himself in, though I do not expect that."

"In the meantime," continued Norvell. "I will ask you to check with all of the Williamsburg silversmiths about the rings and I will see whether anyone can account for the time Mr. Chiswell returned to his lodgings in Williamsburg."

* * *

William and Luck arrived back in Williamsburg in the late evening, both tired from the long ride. Norvell left for his own lodgings in Williamsburg and Luck took his horse to the Wythe stables and entered the back of the main building. Wythe was still up and in his Library. He asked if Key had any supper and when told no, he asked his servant to bring some cold foods and ale for Key.

They sat around a small table in the library and Wythe listened while Luck recounted their trip. The rings seemed like the most damning evidence thought Wythe. Why would Edmund Chiswell have risked the rings being seen by someone and connecting them to James Johnson? Perhaps he just thought that very unlikely.

"Well you have done a great deal of work," said Wythe. "If you are correct about the rings and if Mr. Chiswell's alibi is shaky, then it looks likely that he is the guilty party. My neighbor Robert Carter says that Chiswell has a bad temper and we witnessed that during the debate over the Stamp Act Resolves. I do not welcome the thought of a trial, however. The timing of seeing Chiswell's Roan horse depends upon Jacob's word and a jury may not accept a slave's word against Chiswell—right or wrong. It is possible he will come up with an alternative explanation for having the rings, but that will be the major hurdle. Still, all of the evidence is circumstantial. A jury may not be willing to convict based on that evidence."

Luck went to bed troubled. He was sure that Edmund Chiswell was guilty, but what if they could not prove it? Would Chiswell get away with it? And what is the connection to the Treasury investigation? That also seems unresolved. Perhaps Mr. Wythe will figure that out. After all, the Treasury issue may suggest a motive, but the actions of Speaker Robinson with regard to his lending practices are not really part of the murder investigation. He supposed the House of Burgesses would be responsible for examining the lending issue.

CHAPTER 24

Saturday June 1

Sheriff Norvell came by the Wythe house a bit after eight and having had no breakfast Wythe invited him to join them at the dining table. Luck too had just made an appearance and Wythe noted that both Luck and William seemed tired and drawn. The long trip the last two days and the startling revelations had undoubtedly caused both a restless night.

As usual, Elizabeth Wythe had Lydia lay out a nice breakfast buffet of cold and hot foods that her husband liked; she suspected the men would be hungry and somewhat dispirited after the events of yesterday, which George had shared with her last night before going to bed. She found the investigation interesting and was most surprised that Edmund Chiswell would have stolen rings intended for James Johnson's daughter. She felt that was mean spirited, depriving Mr. Johnson's daughter an important remembrance of her father.

No one seemed to want to talk about the case during breakfast and so they discussed a variety of events and issues facing Virginia and Williamsburg. Norvell had not been at the House of Burgesses during the Stamp Act debates and was interested in Wythe's opinion on what is likely to occur over the next few years.

"That is a good question, William," said Wythe. "I expect we are going to see continued opposition to the Stamp Act, perhaps civil disobedience, with people simply refusing to use the stamps. That will raise issues as to what is legal or not, and you may be in the cross-hairs over the enforcement issue."

"Well, at least I don't have the responsibility of collecting the Stamp Act tax." said Norvell. "I expect that whoever agrees to take that on will be regarded with disdain by many here in Virginia, though I expect the more conservative elements will support the position of the Crown and not offer opposition."

"It may be that if there is wide-spread opposition in all of the colonies, we might see Parliament reconsider," suggested Wythe. "But there are some in Parliament that want to ensure the relative positions of Parliament and the colonial legislatures. It is a matter of principle, both for them, but also for us. That is the prescription for continued conflict."

"We all seem to be avoiding the investigation," continued Wythe. "I am so disappointed that the guilty party looks like a fellow member of the House of Burgesses. That really is shocking and unfortunately the issue of the use of Treasury funds is likely the motive for the murder, so I am afraid we are opening Pandora's Box—this is likely to do considerable damage to the reputation of Speaker Robinson. Yesterday, Robert Carter confirmed that there was concern in the Governor's Council about the financial dealings and also noted that he had witnessed Edmund Chiswell's temper, which I was not aware of before his interactions with Patrick Henry on Monday."

"Ultimately," said Norvell, "whether Speaker Robinson has misused Treasury funds is not the crux of the case. Yes, it goes to motive, but the motive would be there whether or not the rumors are true. It is unlikely that James Johnson had access to more information than many of the other Burgesses on the special committee, but he might have thought he had inside information. It is possible that Mr. Page might have discovered something on his own and told Johnson without informing other members of the investigating committee, but I am doubtful."

"I would like to talk to John Page, but he has left town and I am not anxious for another long ride to see him. I know that Page and Tom Jefferson were close, roommates at William and Mary, so I might ask Tom to make that trip if necessary, or I might send a messenger with a letter asking Mr. Page to clarify his discussions both with Mr. Johnson and Mr. Chiswell. We should talk to Mrs. McIntyre to see if she or any other lodger can substantiate Edmund Chiswell's claim to be back shortly after eleven—I will do that," continued Norvell.

"Luck would you go back to silversmith James Craig and see if he has a drawing of the rings and whether he made similar rings for Chiswell. If he did not, as I expect he did not, then ask him whether any other jewelers would have the capability and might have made a similar set of rings. And then check around to see if any of the other silversmiths made similar rings."

"The rings are certainly the most damming evidence," said Wythe. "Mr. Chiswell might come up with an alternative reason for their being in his possession, but since he did not have one yesterday, any subsequent rationale is suspect."

"Let's meet at Chowning's Tavern at three and compare notes." said Norvell, "We can also see if Josiah Chowning can provide any better timeline on that Sunday evening."

✳ ✳ ✳

Luck left and walked down the Duke of Gloucester Street to the silversmith James Craig's shop. Fortunately he was in and agreed to make a rough sketch of the inter-twinning rings, if Key promised to return it, as it was Craig's own unique design and he did not want to share it with other silversmiths.

When Craig had finished with the sketch, Key was sure that these were the rings that Mary Chiswell had on that she said had been given to her by her husband the previous week. When asked, Mr. Craig said that he had not made a similar set of rings for Mr. Chiswell and had made only one other such set, a couple of years ago for another merchant here in Williamsburg, the owner of Raleigh Tavern. He had said that it was a present for his wife.

Luck thanked James Craig, and since the silversmith's shop was near the Raleigh Tavern, he hoped he could have a brief word with the owner to confirm the possession of the similar rings. Fortunately, Anthony Hay, the owner of the Tavern, was available.

"Yes," said Hay, "the sketch looks very much like the rings I bought a couple of years ago for my wife—a Christmas present. She loves them and it was a good expenditure of money. They are unique; I have not seen any others like them."

"Could your wife have misplaced the rings or given them to someone else in the family perhaps?" asked Key.

"No," replied Hay. "She still has the rings and wears them almost every day unless they would interfere with work she might be doing. If you want to ask her, I am sure she would show you the rings."

"Thank you for the offer. It probably is not necessary but I will check with Sheriff Norvell," replied Key. Luck left the Raleigh Tavern convinced that it was likely that the rings worn by Mary Chiswell were unique and likely bought by James Johnson for his daughter Bethany.

The only other silversmith shop that James Craig felt had the skill to make such a ring was the Geddy Silversmiths and Key went there next and spoke with Mr. George Geddy.

"That is a lovely ring design," said Geddy. "I recognize and admire James Craig's workmanship. I have not made anything comparable and I don't know of any other silversmith in Williamsburg that has done so or even would have the technical skills to do so."

❋ ❋ ❋

Norvell rode over to Mrs. McIntyre's guest house and lodgings to see if she could provide any further amplification of Edmund

Chiswell's actions and the timing of them. Mrs. Lucy McIntyre was a widow and like many widows, used her home for boarders to earn enough money to keep going. As the House of Burgesses was not in session, Mrs. McIntyre had only one lodger at this time. "How can I help you Sheriff?" asked Mrs. McIntyre. She was in her early 50s and still quite attractive. The Sheriff had seen her a few times before and they knew each other, but were not close friends, though he remembered that she has a keen sense of humor.

"I am following up on the movements of Edmund Chiswell, one of your guests, on the Sunday evening twelve days ago, the night of the murder of James Johnson." said Norvell. "A Roan horse matching the description of the one that Mr. Chiswell rode was seen near the murder site. However, he claims that he returned to your lodgings about eleven that evening. I know you are unlikely to keep track of everyone's coming and going, but I am hoping you might have noticed when Chiswell returned on Sunday night."

"My role does not include monitoring guests' comings and goings," said Mrs. McIntyre. "I imagine if I did that, I would have fewer guests staying with me. And in any case, I retire to my own rooms about ten in the evening and go to sleep shortly thereafter."

"I can understand your reticence," said Norvell, "but this is a murder investigation. Someone made Mrs. Johnson, who has a young daughter, a widow and perhaps you might reconsider if you know anything."

"I am sore sorry for Mrs. Johnson's loss," said Mrs. McIntyre. "I really did not hear anything. However, at breakfast the next morning, one of the lodgers—I do not remember which one —kidded Mr. Chiswell about coming in so late at night, or as he put it, 'so early this morning.' That would seem to suggest that Mr. Chiswell might have not returned here until after midnight."

"Thank you for that information. I will need a list of all of your lodgers that Sunday night," said Norvell. "I promise I will not bother them unless it is absolutely necessary." Mrs. McIntyre provided Norvell with names and addresses for those who lodged with her the night of the murder.

"Would you like to come in for some cake and coffee?" asked Mrs. McIntyre with a twinkle in her eye and a smile on her lips. "The cakes are just out of the oven and there are plenty. You look a bit tired from all of your hard work!"

"Perhaps another time Lucy," said the Sheriff. "I had a large breakfast and don't really have the time now. But I promise I will come back another time and take you up on your offer. When I am in Williamsburg, I don't do much cooking for myself and tend to eat at one of the taverns in town."

"I can certainly provide better food than you can find in a tavern," said Mrs. McIntyre. "All of my borders say my meals are what brings them back. Let me provide you with an open invitation to come enjoy some of my cooking!"

"Thank you, Lucy" said Norvell. "I promise to do so in the future. But I will certainly let you know in advance."

"I look forward to having you at my table soon," Lucy said as Norvell was leaving.

Norvell next checked to see if John Page was still in town or if he had left to go to his home in Gloucester County. He had come back for the Johnson Inquest and was here for the Stamp Act debates on Monday, but as the business of the House of Burgesses had concluded, he thought Mr. Page had probably left for his home plantation—or perhaps to see his new fiancé. As he expected, Page had left. John Page represented Gloucester County, which was on the other side of the York River. It would be as long a ride as the one to Mr. Chiswell's plantation, and not one that Norvell was anxious to make.

If it is necessary, I will need to make that trip or ask Jefferson if he would be willing, thought Norvell. I could send Key or a messenger, but Mr. Page may feel more comfortable with me or Jefferson doing the questioning. I am sure he is unaware that whatever he told James Johnson might have played some role in the murder and, when he finds that out, he is likely to be distraught about it.

* * *

Norvell joined Key and Wythe at Chowning's at three as planned. They each updated the others on information received. "So it looks like Mr. Chiswell's alibi is not solid," said Norvell, "and the rings worn by his wife Mary were clearly the rings that James Johnson had bought for his daughter Bethany. I think we have enough to bring Edmund Chiswell back to Williamsburg for further questioning and in the meantime, we can track down the few miscellaneous pieces of information to conclude our case."

One question had to do with the timing on the night of the murder and so they asked Josiah Chowning to join them. "Did you have any more thoughts about the night of the murder," asked Norvell. "Specifically, can you be more exact as to when Edmund Chiswell left the premises?"

"As I told your deputy Mr. Key last week," Chowning said. "It was about eleven, though perhaps a bit after eleven when I closed down the Tavern. I always try to close about eleven, other than on Friday and Saturday nights. But I don't like to throw anyone out who is enjoying my fine food and drink. I do remember that Mr. Chiswell was one of the last patrons to leave and it might have been somewhat after eleven, perhaps half twelve. I seem to remember getting to sleep later than usual. It does take me about a half hour to clean up and close down the tavern, though I can do some of that while a few of the patrons are still here.

"Unfortunately, as I told Mr. Key," he continued, "I did not hear anything coming from the direction of the Powder Magazine. My bedroom is in the upstairs and toward the back, so it would have been difficult for me to have heard any conflict occurring there."

"Is there anything else Sheriff?" asked Chowning. When Nor-

180

vell indicated that was all they needed to know, Chowning excused himself and went back to his duties as host of the tavern.

"I would like to know what John Page thinks he knows about the Treasury funds," said Wythe, "and whether he told his suspicions to Johnson. That seems to be the basis for thinking he might be able to leverage a loan from Robinson. At this point that seems the only likely motive, unless we hear something different from Mr. Chiswell."

"But why kill Johnson?" asked Key. "Couldn't Mr. Chiswell have persuaded the Speaker to come up with some funds to help Johnson? The murder seems so unnecessary."

"Possibly Speaker Robinson had no other resources to make the loan, or perhaps he felt that the information was coming out anyway," said Wythe.

"But Edmund Chiswell may have felt differently. He would be involved in a scandal that would affect him and his sister Susanna. There may be serious financial issues that could ruin or severely damage both Speaker Robinson and Mr. Chiswell. But all of this is speculation, unless Chiswell admits to the murder and provides a reason—which I somehow doubt he will."

They were talking and enjoying dinner, when Henry, Speaker Robinson's butler, came into the Chowning's Tavern, asking for the Sheriff. "I am over here, Henry," said Norvell. "What do you need me for?"

"Speaker Robinson asked me to give you this letter," said Henry, and he handed the letter to Norvell. The Sheriff opened the envelope and felt a shock. The envelope contained the rings previously worn by Mary Chriswell and a note. Norvell read the note and passed it around to Wythe and Key.

"Dear Sheriff Norvell, I am sorry to inform you that my brother-in-law, Edmund Chiswell, died last night from injuries suffered while cleaning his pistol—a terrible accident. Mary Chiswell asks that the enclosed rings be provided to Mrs. Johnson, as she feels she may have received them in error. I would appreciate your discretion in this matter. Sincerely,

"Is there a message back to Speaker Robinson?" asked Henry.

"You can tell him that I appreciated the courtesy of the information and I am very sorry for his loss," said Norvell. "I think that is all for the moment." Norvell also looked closely at the rings and saw the engraved rosebud on the inside of each of them.

"What do we do now?" asked Key.

"I would suggest another drink and then heading home," said Wythe. "It looks to me like the investigation is over."

"Well do we now know the truth?" asked Key.

"What exactly is the truth?" mused Norvell out loud. "What do we know for sure? I am not going to charge a dead man for a crime. And I believe that Speaker Robinson is blameless for the murder, if not for other irregularities, which are not the scope of our investigation. Sometimes, you have to just accept things as they are."

"However, Mrs. Johnson deserves knowledge about what we suspect, if cannot prove," continued Norvell. "And Bethany needs to have these rings from her father. I don't think we need to tell her exactly how we received them, but that they came to our attention during the investigation. Luck, if Mr. Wythe agrees, perhaps you and I ought to ride out to their plantation tomorrow and provide them with information that we feel we can share."

"Of course I agree," said Wythe. "They need to have some closure to this dreadful business."

"Luck," asked Norvell, "would you stop by and see Jacob and let him know that he is no longer considered a suspect in the murder? I am sure that will be a relief to him and to Mr. Anderson."

"Yes, I will do so," said Key.

Luck walked over to the blacksmith's shop, which was not far from Chowning's Tavern. He saw Mr. Anderson who came over to see what he wanted. Luck saw Jacob looking across at them apprehensively.

"I have some good news for Jacob," said Key. "Sheriff Norvell has concluded the investigation into the murder of James Johnson and Jacob is in the clear. In fact, it was his description of a horse that he had seen near the Powder Magazine that led us to the person responsible."

Mr. Anderson motioned Jacob over and said "Mr. Key has some good news for you, Jacob. You are in the clear and actually helped Mr. Key and the Sheriff solve the mystery of who murdered Mr. Johnson. While I never doubted your story, it is nice to have a resolution of the matter."

Jacob was overwhelmed, tears streaming down his face. "Thank you very much Mr. Key. Thank you both for believing in me." Jacob then went back to work and Mr. Anderson asked Key who was responsible.

"I think that information should come from the Sheriff, but he wanted to let Jacob know immediately to take any shadow away from him," said Key, who thanked Mr. Anderson and left the shop.

As he walked back to the Wythe house, Luck thought about all that he had learned and yet all that was still unknown. It was evening and George and Elizabeth Wythe had gone next door to the Carter's for supper. Lydia asked Luck if he would like to have an informal supper in the kitchen. "It will just be me as the other servants have already eaten," she said.

"That is very kind of you," said Luck. "And please call me by my first name, I don't really feel comfortable with you calling me Mr. Key and you have been such a help to me in my first two weeks here with Mr. Wythe."

"Oh, I couldn't do that," said Liddy. "It would just not be right. I am a servant and a slave. You have a professional position, even though a junior position, and deserve the respect of being called Mr. Key."

They spent an hour or so in casual conversation. Liddy was aware that the case had been resolved, at least to the Sheriff's satisfaction, and Liddy was happy that Jacob was now freed of any responsibility for the death of Mr. Johnson.

"How did you come to work here for Mr. Wythe?" asked Key.

"I was born into slavery at a plantation in southern Virginia," said Liddy. "My mother died when I was just a girl of about seven. I didn't know who my father was, but rumors said he was the plantation overseer who took advantage of my mother. We worked very hard in the tobacco fields and lived in squalid conditions. I remember crying a lot and being threatened by the overseer. Then a good thing happened. The plantation owners sold me to Master Richard Taliaferro, Mrs. Elizabeth's father, and I became her maid and helpmate, though I had to be taught everything. Both Master Richard and Elizabeth were very kind to me and I began to assume more responsibility as I grew up, When Elizabeth married Mr. Wythe, she asked that I come with her and her father agreed."

"Now by law," continued Liddy, "I am Mr. Wythe's slave, but of course he would not sell me because of Elizabeth. I feel comfortable here. I have a small room to myself, next to the kitchen and they both see to any needs I might have."

"But you are not free," said Luck. "Is that not something that you wish for?"

"Of course," answered Liddy. "Mr. Wythe has indicated that he will free me and provide financial support for me. But I am in no rush for this. Where would I go? And I love Mr. and Mrs. Wythe. They are my family and now you are part of my family. I take care of the household finances with Mrs. Elizabeth and have a budget for certain items and support for the other servants. They always give me a bit more than I really need and when I go through the accounting with her, she tells me to keep the balance and help build up my own financial reserve, so that when I am freed, I will be able to take care of myself."

"So yes," continued Liddy. "I hope that I eventually can say I am a free black woman and not a slave. If I want to be a servant to a family it would be my choice and not because I am owned by someone. I would really like to own my own guest house someday—that would be rare in Virginia for a former slave—

but who knows. I can dream about it and perhaps it will happen in the future."

"I hope you will have that opportunity," said Luck. "You are a remarkable woman. I have really enjoyed our informal conversation. I feel you just know so much more about life than I do. Mr. Wythe has been educating me, but sometimes I feel I just need to hear some practical thinking. May we do this again?"

Liddy agreed and said she also enjoyed talking with Luck. "You are Virginia's future. What you and others like Tom Jefferson do will have a big impact on us all."

✳ ✳ ✳

Later that night Luck sat in Wythe's library talking to him about the investigation. "It doesn't feel like we have unraveled everything," said Key. "There are too many unresolved issues. I wish I felt better about the outcome, but I am not very comfortable with all of the uncertainty surrounding the case. If Mr. Chiswell did murder James Johnson, what was the real reason? Was it over the possible Treasury scandal? Was it over some other matter? We know that Chiswell had a temper. Again, why would Mr. Johnson agree to meet Chiswell in the Powder Magazine?"

"Like you," said Wythe. "I am uncomfortable not knowing the full story. However, I am comforted with the notion that we should not let the perfect become the enemy of the good. Or as Shakespeare said, not to 'strive to better, oft we mar what's well'."

"I'm afraid I do not understand your meaning here," said Luck.

"Well we have a reasonably good result. We know, with near certainty, that Mr. Chiswell was the murderer. That knowledge will bring some closure to the Johnson family. We have retrieved the rings intended for Bethany Johnson, again a good result. She will remember her father when she wears the rings."

"What more do we need to know to attain a perfect result?"

asked Wythe. "If we find out that the motive was blackmail —silence for a loan—that can only harm the reputation of Mr. Johnson, which will damage his family's good thoughts about him and perhaps how others view him. If we prove the blackmail had to do with improper Treasury practices of Speaker Robinson, we will blacken his name and perhaps others. If in fact there are irregularities in the Treasury accounts I expect they will be uncovered by the current special committee of the House of Burgesses."

"Finally," said Wythe, "we have to keep in mind the position of Sheriff Norvell, who works closely with the Speaker. Any additional investigation by him will cause him pain and possible censure by others. So we have a result that is good, if not a perfect resolution of the case."

"I really had not thought that through," said Luck. "I am so indebted to you and the Sheriff for allowing me to be involved in this case. It has widened my understanding of Williamsburg, of Virginia politics and human nature itself."

"Luck, I am very happy to have you as my new junior clerk," said Wythe. "I am not sure I can promise you the same level of excitement as you have experienced these last two weeks, but I look forward to your participation in the legal issues that I deal with and further discussions with you, Tom Jefferson and others on the future of Virginia. In many ways, it is the next generation, you and Tom, who have to sort our path forward."

They said good night and headed to their rooms, George to go over the events of the day with Elizabeth and Luck to read some more from the book by John Locke that he had borrowed from the library.

CHAPTER 25

Sunday June 2

Another early morning ride to the Johnson Plantation Rosebud. Sheriff Norvell picked Luck Key up at seven and they headed to the Johnson Plantation. On the way they discussed what to tell Mrs. Johnson and what to hold in reserve.

"We don't want to unnecessarily add additional grief to the either the Johnson or Robinson Families," said Norvell. "My thought is to tell the Johnsons that we have come to the conclusion about the murderer, Edmund Chiswell, but as he has died, we cannot bring him before a judge and jury, so there will always be some doubt as to the motive and exactly what happened. We can say that there is evidence that Mr. Chiswell or Mr. Johnson had set a meeting at the Powder Magazine and that some altercation led to Johnson's death."

"Since we are not able to question Edmund Chiswell, we do not know for sure why James Johnson and Mr. Chiswell agreed to meet, whether their business was personal or financial. Thus, the motive for the meeting and the killing are, at this time, only conjecture. We have no evidence and do not believe any other party is to blame in the death. So it seems to me, the simpler the explanation, the better," concluded Norvell.

"Your judgment and experience in these matters is much greater than mine," said Key, "but I had an extensive conversation with George Wythe about the status of the case last night and with further thinking have come to the same conclusion. How do we explain the rings?"

"We can tell Mrs. Johnson," said Norvell, "that in the course of our investigations, we became aware that Mr. Johnson had commissioned the rings from silversmith James Craig, for Bethany's birthday. We were able to retrieve the rings and felt like the two ladies would like to have them. They are already paid for and what they decide to do with the rings is totally up to them."

"Well, I hope Bethany receives them," said Key. "It would be a cherished reminder of the love her father had for her. Though given their financial difficulties, it may be they will have to sell them."

"I hope not," said Norvell. "I frankly am worried about how they will handle things alone. I don't fully trust the Overseer Mechem to always act in their best interests."
They arrived at the plantation about one in the afternoon, and were met by the same servant, Samuel, who took care of their horses the previous times they were there. Norvell thanked him for again seeing to the horses and asked if they could speak with Mrs. Johnson. Samuel showed them into the parlor.

"William and Mr. Key, we were not expecting you today. To what do we owe this pleasure?" asked Mrs. Johnson. She was wearing a simple black frock and no jewelry other than pearl neckless that she had worn before.

"I am afraid this is not a pleasure call, though I regret that, and hope our coming is not too unpleasant for you," said Norvell.

"Of course not," said Mrs. Johnson. "Are you here to tell us about some progress in the murder investigation?"

"Yes," said Norvell. "We do have news."

"Let me see if I can find Bethany," said Mrs. Johnson. She left and shortly returned with Bethany, who seemed to have been working in the garden, given how she was dressed.

"I am so sorry to be so casually dressed," said Bethany. "I did not know you were coming today, or I would have dressed accordingly. But with fewer servants now, I am trying to take care of our kitchen garden. I must look a mess!"

Luck thought she looked quite beautiful in any dress, but only said "You have no reason to apologize. We are the ones who came unannounced."

"Let me quickly get our business done," said Norvell. "We have an update on our investigation. We believe that your husband met Edmund Chiswell about midnight on the morning of May 20. We are not sure exactly why, but there may have been some financial matter between them. There was an altercation and Chiswell killed your husband. Unfortunately, Chiswell is also now dead, perhaps an accident or by his own hand, so we are unable to question him to find out about details and motive."

"That is terrible. I did not know Mr. Chiswell, other than by reputation, so this comes as a great surprise," said Mrs. Johnson. "So where does the investigation go from here."

"Frankly, I think this is the end of the investigation," said Norvell.

"We are reasonably sure that Mr. Chiswell committed the murder and we may never know the full motive or why your husband agreed to meet him in the Powder Magazine. I am not sure that further investigation will benefit you or anyone," said the Sheriff.

"We have one other item," said Key. "In the course of our investigation, we came into possession of a set of inter-twined rings. I tracked them down to the maker, silversmith James Craig, and he told us that Mr. Johnson had bought the rings as a gift for Bethany's sixteenth birthday, which I suppose is coming soon. I am sure you will want to have these."

Luck gave the rings to Mrs. Johnson who looked at them with tears in her eyes and handed them to Bethany. "They are beautiful," she said. "How thoughtful of father to buy these for me. I hope to keep them in memory of him."

William and Luck stood up to leave, but Mrs. Johnson would not hear of their leaving so soon. "You are tired from your long ride here as are your horses," said Sarah. "Please stay and have dinner with us. It will not be as sumptuous perhaps as last Sunday, when we prepared for your coming, but I am sure it will be satisfying and give you a chance to rest a bit."

"That is very kind of you, and if we will be no trouble, we accept," said William. "If you will have Samuel check my pack on the back of my horse, he will find a bottle of Burgundy that came for me when the ship *Hope* docked early last week, I realize this is not a celebration, but at least you might view it as a conclusion, and perhaps a start of the next chapter in your lives."

Bethany excused herself and went upstairs to wash and dress, as she was wearing her gardening clothes. Samuel brought the wine and Sarah asked William to open it so they could have a glass. The French wine was full-bodied, with a mild fruit flavor, but smooth and relatively dry. Sarah proclaimed the wine a success and left the men to their wine while she went to the kitchen to see to the preparation of the dinner. She had already planned on a chicken, and with lettuce that Bethany had picked from their garden they would have a salad and fried potatoes with onions, which had been one of her husband's favorite dishes.

It was hard now for Sarah to think of her husband in the past tense. He had always been there for her and without his guidance she was unsure if they would be able to keep the plantation. She did not trust Mr. Mechem, whom she saw as overbearing and condescending. But at least he appeared to have nothing to do with her husband's death.

Bethany came downstairs and was beautifully dressed in a simple tan frock, with a dark brown shawl. She had on a black arm-ban in remembrance of her father. William asked if she would like a glass of the Burgundy and when she said yes, poured one for her. After a couple of sips, she said it was delightful and then excused herself to see if she could be of any help to her mother.

"I wonder if they have had to sell some more slaves," asked Luck. "I suspect their financial situation is somewhat more difficult now. I wish there was something I could do to assist them."

Bethany came in and invited Luck and William to the dining room, which was set for the four of them. "You are probably wondering about our reduced level of servants," said Sarah. "Carter Braxton, probably at the urging of his wife, was kind enough to offer to buy a couple of our house slaves to help us in our fiscal difficulty, including our cook, whom they coveted. I really am grateful to the Braxtons but I don't know where to go to for assistance right now. I wish I trusted Mr. Mechem more, but I am worried that he is more interested in his own position than in assisting us to find a resolution to ours."

"I am very happy to assist you," said William. "Now that the case is closed, I should have time to come out here later this week, perhaps on Friday, and be able to work a couple of days on the finances and see if I can come up with some ideas that might be helpful for you." Sarah replied that next Friday would be fine and asked him to stay at the manor house when he came.

The dinner was delightful, even if the situation was a bit sad, because of the outcome. Luck enjoyed chatting with Bethany and they seemed to have an easy companionship with each other. He knew he was in no position to 'court' Bethany, given his fiscal situation. However, her gentle smile and manner gave him some hopes.
They talked and enjoyed one another's company for a few hours, when William indicated that they should be on their way, given the long ride ahead. He promised Sarah that he would come back on Friday. Sarah was very appreciative and said she looked forward to seeing him again.

On the way back, both William and Luck were thinking about the day and the future. "I certainly have enjoyed working with you," said Key. "You have given me great insight into working with people. It has been an exciting case and I imagine my work as junior clerk to Mr. Wythe will not be quite as stimulating."

"There are many things you can learn from Mr. Wythe," said Norvell, "and you have proved a great help to me. Maybe you

will want to follow in Tom Jefferson's wake and become a lawyer—not that we need more," Norvell joked. "I too have enjoyed
your assistance and be assured that if a similar need occurs I
will be calling on you again." Luck thanked him.

They arrived at Wythe's home late at night and Norvell said
goodbye to Key and asked him to give his regards to Mr. Wythe.
The night was warm and after stabling his horse, he walked over
to the Wythe home. What an adventure this has been thought
Luck. He committed himself to doing whatever was necessary
to please George Wythe, but hoped that the future brought
more opportunities to work with Sheriff Norvell.

Luck mused about his future. Mr. Wythe had suggested that
he prepare himself and be ready for future opportunities and
seemed pleased with his work. Who knows what the future will
bring? He was only eighteen and now the possibilities seemed
greater than ever. He would not be a farmer like his father and
hoped he would have other challenges and opportunities to
prove himself to other people.

Sheriff William Norvell also was considering his own future.
Edmund Chiswell's death had saved him from having to arrest
a prominent person with a potentially ugly trial ahead—so he
did not risk his reputation against the conservative plantation
society. He also wondered about his feelings for Sarah Johnson.
It had been ten years since the death of his wife and perhaps it
was time to think about getting married again. Could he help
Sarah figure out a way forward to keep the plantation? It might
be an impossible task but one that he thought was worth the
effort. He also had enjoyed working with young Mr. Key. Perhaps they would find a way to work together again.

CHAPTER 25

Epilogue

Speaker John Robinson died the following year in 1766. Because of rumors concerning his handling of Treasury accounts, and because Robinson was widely considered one of the colony's richest men, the supervising judges appointed three executors and required an unprecedented bond of £250,000. Peyton Randolph, as executor for the estate, placed notices in the Virginia Gazette, and other venues, asking that all people in debt to Robinson "make immediate payment."

Colonial Treasury records confirmed that Speaker Robinson had been using the paper money he was supposed to destroy (in his role as Treasurer), and also lending out taxes collected by local sheriffs before depositing them in the Treasury. Robinson lent the currency to his political supporters, as well as to pay his personal debts. In December 1766, a staggering report to the House of Burgesses indicated that Robinson's estate owed the colony over £100,000. After the Robinson financial scandal, the roles of speaker and treasurer were separated.

Records also indicated that the three executors had all owed Robinson money as had key members of the committees appointed by the House of Burgesses to investigate Robinson, undoubtedly a factor in the earlier whitewashing of the issue. Burgesses William Byrd III was the largest debtor owing £15,000 to the estate. Despite pressure from the House of Burgesses to settle the estate, by November 1769, the administrators had only repaid the Treasury about £21,000, and acknowledged a debt of a further £101,508, so Pendleton liquidated Robinson's former residence and sold his slaves, although he allowed Robinson's widow, who had married Colonel Griffin, to purchase considerable amounts at the estate sale, without requiring security. The largest debtor Byrd eventually had to sell a large land holding that eventually became downtown Richmond, Va. in order to satisfy the debt.

The Robinson estate was also owed £8,085 by the Lead Mine Company, a venture by Robinson, Governor Fauquier, Byrd and Robinson's father-in-law John Chiswell, to develop lead deposits along the New River in what later became Wythe County, Virginia. John Chiswell had discovered the outcroppings in 1756, and Byrd established a fort during the French and Indian war to protect that area, but it had not been developed before Robinson's death. After Virginia declared its independence, the Commonwealth operated the lead mine, which became an important military supplier for the patriot cause. In a drink-fueled dispute over the Lead Mine Company, Chiswell stabbed Robert Routledge in a tavern and later committed suicide, rather than face justice.

The estate was not closed until 1808, and the then executor Edmond Pendleton's decision to pay debts owed Virginia in depreciated currency generated controversy and produced a famous legal decision concerning federal-state relations. *Page v. Pendleton* was decided by the then Judge George Wythe. He held that the federal treaty with Great Britain, under the U.S. Constitution, superseded state law, and thus allowed the payment to settle the debt.

Notes and Acknowledgments

George Wythe (1726-1806) is one of least known but most important founding fathers and perhaps the most influential teacher in American history for his mentorship of Thomas Jefferson, and his legal training of Chief Justice John Marshall, James Monroe, Henry Clay and others. In all, Wythe taught two presidents, a vice president, five secretaries of state, two US Supreme Court justices and attorneys general, seven governors and numerous high ranking cabinet officers and public officials. His thinking so influenced Thomas Jefferson that a space on the Declaration of Independence was left blank so George Wythe's name would appear first among the Virginia signors of the document. Before his death he had freed most of his slaves, and after his death freed the remaining ones, providing funds for all of them on their release and in his will upon his death, living up to the spirit of the Declaration. His devoted housekeeper, Liddy Broadnax, as a free black woman, stayed with Elizabeth and George Wythe until their deaths. He had bought her a house and provided ongoing financial support for her in his will.

William Norvell (1725-1802) was Sheriff of Williamsburg and James City County from 1757 to 1769 and was a Vestryman at Burton Church. He was a representative at the last Royal Burgesses in 1775 and a delegate to the Virginia State Convention in 1775 and 1776. In his will, he freed all of his slaves. His family in the book is fictional.

Luck Key (1744/7-1830) is the author's fourth great-grandfather and after his apprenticeship he did become a farmer like his father, first in Virginia, then North Carolina and finally settling in Richburg, South Carolina, where he changed the spelling of his name to Kee, because "there were too many Keys," in South Carolina. His son Martin Kee had 17 children and their descendants are spread throughout the United States.

Robert Carter III, guided by his faith and his concerns for social justice, engaged in his lifetime the largest manumission and release of slaves prior to the Civil War. He freed more than 500 African-Americans and provided funds for them. This was strongly opposed by his heirs and other Virginia plantation owners, at one time he and his wife had to flee for their lives. To illustrate his religious conversion and break the generational cycle of slavery in his family, he erected a large pulpit in front of his home and announced the freedom of his remaining 452 slaves in 1791: *I have for some time past been convinced that to retain them in slavery is contrary to the true Principles of Religion and Justice, and that therefore it was my Duty to manumit them.* Carter implemented an immediate yet gradual emancipation, so they could remain as employees (if they chose) in order to become self-sufficient. He is buried in an unmarked grave in the garden at his family home Nomony at the Great Neck of Virginia.

James Johnson, his wife Sarah and daughter Bethany, and the Overseer John Mechem are fictional characters.

Edmond Chiswell and his wife Mary are fictional characters. Susanna Chiswell was the daughter of Col. John Chiswell of Hanover County and she did marry Speaker John Robinson. However, she had no brother.

Most of the other main characters in the book are historical figures and the author has attempted to provide them with dialogue consistent with their lives. However, everything related to the murder is fictional as are the characters' interactions about the murder and other events in the book. The character of John Page is a composite of two related individuals.

Many biographies of George Wythe are out of print, but two books were very helpful in providing a context for his extraordinary life:

Jefferson's Godfather, The Man Behind the Man, Suzanne Harman Munson.

Jefferson's Second Father, The Life and Strange Death of Chancellor Wythe, signer of the Declaration of Independence, John Bailey

The author has incorporated their descriptions of people and events where relevant to the book.

The Marshall-Wythe School of Law at the College of William and Mary houses a collection of articles and items about George Wythe, including a description and duplication of his library. Thomas Jefferson, when governor of Virginia, created the College of William and Mary Law School and George Wythe became its first Professor of Law. The George Wythe Room in the Wolf Library is the depository of Wythe information: https://lawlibrary.wm.edu/wythepedia/index.php/George_Wythe_Room .

Colonial Williamsburg is a national treasure www.colonialwilliamsburg.org. The author has attempted to be accurate on the streets and structures of historical Williamsburg, but has taken some liberties. The Courthouse on Duke of Gloucester Street was not yet build in 1765, but the author wanted to use it as the site of the Johnson Inquest. Any inaccuracies are the fault of the author and not anyone connected to Colonial Williamsburg or its Foundation.

The debate over the Stamp Act Resolves actually took place on Wednesday, May 29. There is no official record of the debate, and Patrick Henry's remarks (though widely accepted) are only alluded to by a French observer who had recorded his thoughts about the debate.

Sarah Jane Chesney's master thesis, "Propagating Stature: Gentlemen Planters and their Greenhouses in the Eighteenth-Century Chesapeake." The College of William and Mary, January 2009, provided excellent information on greenhouses in the Tidewater region, https://scholarworks.wm.edu/cgi/viewcontent.cgi?article=5995&context=etd.

For a discussion of African-Americans serving the function of overseer or driver, see, William E. Wiethoff "Enslaved Africans' Rivalry with White Overseers in Plantation Culture: An Unconventional Interpretation," *Journal of Black Studies*, Vol.36 (3), p.429-455 (2006).

The author would like to thank several people who read and commented on various drafts of the book. Two of my siblings, Tracy Elizabeth Kee Christopher and Terry M. Kee (and Terry's spouse Debra Billings-Kee) read early drafts and gave me a number of suggestions that I incorporated into the book. My former colleague at George Washington University, Dr. Kathryn Newcomer did a final review and was very encouraging. My spouse, Suzanne Erlon Kee read every word and chapter numerous times, and made many corrections and suggestions. She was supportive throughout the effort and I could not have completed it without her invaluable help. My son, James J. Kee provided me with a number of useful suggestions and assisted in the front cover design.

About the Author

James Edwin Kee is Professor Emeritus of Public Policy and Administration, George Washington University. He joined GW in 1985 after a career in government policy and administration, working in a variety of roles: legal intern to Senator Robert Kennedy, Counsel to the New York State Legislature, and Budget and Finance Director of the State of Utah. At GW he served as a department chair, senior associate dean and dean in the School of Business and Public Management. His teaching and research interests at GW included public finance, leadership, intergovernmental relations, and public-private-partnerships. He is the co-author of three academic books and author or co-author of numerous journal articles. He and his spouse Suzanne currently live in Germany (summer, where their son is an opera singer) and Portugal (winter). This is his first book of fiction.

Other books by James Edwin Kee

Out of Balance, with former Utah Governor Scott M. Matheson, Peregrine Smith Book.

Transforming Public and Nonprofit Organizations: Stewardship for Leading Change, with Kathryn E, Newcomer, Berrett-Koehler Publishers.

Governing Cross-Sector Collaboration, with John J. Forrer and Eric Boyer, Jossey Bass.

More on Sheriff William Norvell, George Wythe and Luck Key. A new murder mystery coming in late 2021, set in historic Williamsburg during the Townshend Act protests of 1767. Norvell and Wythe find themselves on opposite sides when dealing with the murder of a local merchant.

If you enjoyed *Murder in the Powder Magazine*, please leave a review with Amazon. Your comments and suggestions are very helpful to a new author.

www.ingramcontent.com/pod-product-compliance
Lightning Source LLC
Chambersburg PA
CBHW071611150726
48000CB00004B/1678